SO YOU TH
MEDIA IS BAD NOW?

Whether you're a big fan of CNN or Fox News, any truly objective person knows that the news media of today is out of control, spinning stories in favor of the various agendas that they advocate.

Yep…it's true.

Now move ahead into the next century to a time when the news might not be reported anymore, but "predicted"—and the more sensational the prediction, the greater the readership. But obviously to do well, any good newspaper would want to make their predictions stick…right? Well that's the way it was with the members of "The Fourth Estate," the small group of elite journalists who made the news "happen," whether by manipulation of facts, bribery, blackmail, or even in some cases—assassination. But in the year 2103, it occurred to some journalists that there might be a better way. Unfortunately, thinking like that could land you on the wrong end of a death notice prediction…

FOR A SECOND COMPLETE NOVEL, TURN TO PAGE 79

CAST OF CHARACTERS

McCLEOD
As the ace reporter on the Star-Times, it was his job not only to predict the news, but to make sure it happened!

TRACY
For someone who was nothing more than her paper's prime co-respondent, she sure seemed to know a lot—about everything.

OVERMAN
This hard-driving newspaper editor didn't care how dire or unethical his news predictions were, as long as they came true.

WAINWRIGHT
As McCleod's main competition, he relished the idea of making his adversary the subject of his paper's latest news prediction.

CRIPPS
He was well liked and thought of as a good reporter, but he had the bad habit of not always making sure his stories came "true."

MAYOR SPURGESS
He wanted to be a good mayor, but he found his agenda was more prediction-driven than he ever thought possible.

NEWSHOUND, 2103 A.D.

By
MILTON LESSER

ARMCHAIR FICTION
PO Box 4369, Medford, Oregon 97504

CHAPTER ONE

DARIUS McLeod leaned back comfortably and watched the mayor sweat.

His Honor popped a phenobarb tablet between his lips, tossing his head and gulping the pill down without water. His moist, nervous hands left their wet imprint on the desktop when he reached into his breast pocket and withdrew a clipping from the morning's *New York World*.

"You people elected me, McLeod," he said. "Now get me out of this mess."

"We merely supported your candidacy, Your Honor," McLeod said easily. "But let's see what you got there."

"It amounts to the same thing," the mayor pleaded. "For God's sake, give me a break."

McLeod shrugged and unfolded the *World* clipping on his desk. "Naturally, the *World* will oppose your administration," he began. "Otherwise they'll never be able to live down the *Star-Times'* scoop on your election."

"That's precisely what I was saying. The way I understand it, you people will have to support your man. The *Star-Times* can't abandon me to the wolves, not now."

"I'm only a reporter," McLeod explained. "We report events, not make them."

"That's it. That's what I mean. The attitude. You're treating me like a child."

"You're acting like one."

"All I want is what's fair. Whatever you think is fair."

"Then let me read this thing." The column clipped from the *World* bore the cut-line COMING EVENTS. McLeod had always enjoyed the *Star-Times'* LOOKING FORWARD

better, although he had to admit that the *World's* cut of a swami rubbing his crystal ball had a certain fundamental appeal for the masses. House-written, the *World* column appeared under the by-line of Nostradamus.

McLeod scanned the printed lines quickly. There was a prediction on the outcome of the World Series. It had better turn out incorrect, thought McLeod; the *Star-Times* had spent a small fortune building up the opposing team. There was something about the dangers of forest fires and an indirect reference to the possibility of a conflagration next week in the Adirondack Game Preserve. (The *Star-Times* would be alerting its fire-fighting unit to prevent such a possibility, McLeod knew.) There was a talk of an impending war between Yugoslavia and France at a time when relations between the two countries were never more harmonious. McLeod wondered how the *World* would ever swing it. He read the last two items aloud.

" 'We think it's high time the mayor of New York be exposed for his corrupt political dealings. We wouldn't be surprised if the mayor was forced to resign his office in January... What ace reporter of what rival New York daily is going to meet with a fatal accident next week? Remember, you read it here first!' "

"January," said the mayor as Darius McLeod folded the column and lit a cigarette. "That's next month."

"That ace reporter stuff, they could be talking about me."

"Eh? If I'm forced to resign, you'll be scooped."

"Yeah, scooped," McLeod mused. "We're their chief rival. I'm the big Huck-a-muck over here. Those dirty sons—they can get me out of the way and scoop us at the same time. Listen, Your Honor, check back with me later. I've got to see the City Editor."

"But I'm not politically corrupt—"

"We'll decide. We'll let you know," Darius McLeod shouted, already running from his glass-walled office and through the clattering din of the City Room, disturbing the milling knot of scribes and gunmen going over last minute instructions from the Crime Editor, shouldering by the line of trim, pretty co-respondents receiving their briefs from the Society Editor, almost knocking down the Medical Editor who was either on the point of finding a cure for the *World's* latest plague or dreaming up one of his own, McLeod didn't remember which.

McLEOD found Overman, the City Editor, perched on a corner of his desk and barking orders into a microphone. "What do you mean, he won't jump? We said he'd jump. Coax him. Push him if you can get away with it, I don't care. Don't make it obvious." Overman cocked his gaunt head to one side, listening to the receiver imbedded in his ear. He looked like a walking ad for hyperthyroid treatment, with bulging eyes, hollow cheeks, and fidgety limbs. He couldn't sit still and he didn't try. "All right, we'll hold up the story. And *you're* the guy who asked for a raise." Overman dropped the microphone hose back into its cubby and looked up. "Sometimes I wonder what the hell they think a reporter draws his salary for. What do you want, Darius?"

"The *World's* gunning for me, chief."

"I already saw it."

"Then don't just sit there."

"What do you want me to do, hold your hand? Of course the *World's* gunning for you. Great story for them, and they also kill off our star reporter in the process. *If* they get away with it."

"Damn it!" McLeod exploded. "This is the twenty-second century. If the *World* says I'm going to meet with a fatal accident, then my life's in danger." McLeod winced at his own words. In a matter of minutes he had been reduced to the mayor's level and he didn't like it.

"Counter-prognostication has already taken steps, Darius. Don't go off the deep end on me. It happens like this every time. Even a top-flight reporter sheds his own sophistication when the story's about himself."

"How do you expect me to take it?"

"Just relax, that's all."

"Maybe you want me to write my own obituary."

"Don't try so hard to be funny. Excuse me." Overman cocked his head again and listened, then pulled out his microphone and barked: "All right, all right. Don't cry. We can't get them all. I'm not saying it was your fault. Report back in."

"What's the matter?" McLeod asked, wanting to know.

"Harry Crippens is the matter. Remember Congressman Horner? That story yesterday?"

McLeod recalled it vaguely. Something about Horner committing suicide unexpectedly.

"Well, he didn't jump. The *World's* Security Forces rescued him and got a scoop. Another wrongo for us, Darius. That's the second story Crippens bungled this month."

"Maybe it wasn't Cripp's fault, chief."

Crippens was a plump, owl-faced man with big, watery eyes swimming behind concave glasses. McLeod had always liked him. He was the grimmest, saddest, cryingest, most logical drunk McLeod had ever met. Wonderful drinking partner.

"I didn't say it was. Just thinking, though."

"If psychology flubbed a dub on Horner, you can't blame Cripp."

"Not what I mean. The *World's* prediction is vague, see? Who's a star reporter? How do you single the man out? Any big by-line guy will do, right?"

"I guess so."

"Crippens gets his share of by-lines, Darius."

"Hey wait a minute—"

"Why spend the time protecting you next week if we don't have to? It's expensive and not a sure thing. We'd hate to lose you, Darius."

"Thank you."

"But Crippens is bungling. He ought to meet the *World's* requirements. We do the job for them the first of next week. They get their story and we keep our number one man—alive. How does it sound?"

"Rotten," McLeod said. "I'm not going to sit by and let Cripp take that kind of rap for me. What kind of louse do you think I am, anyway?"

"Let it simmer, Darius. There's no hurry. I suppose His Honor has been around to use your crying towel?"

McLeod nodded. "That's right."

"I thought he would. It was your series of articles that got him elected in the first place. You saved my life, now support me. One of those deals. It was obvious the *World* would try to show corruption after their own candidate lost."

"Is the *Star-Times* going to protect Mayor Spurgess' record?"

OVERMAN jerked his head from side to side, the stretched, translucent lids blinking over popping eyes. "It's always easier to prove corruption than disprove it, you know that. We'd be backing the wrong animal, Darius. I've got it figured, though."

"How do you mean?"

"They won't have much of a story if something violent happens to the mayor between now and next month. I don't want to see it in LOOKING FORWARD, though. Just make it happen and get the scoop. See? We can't let the mayor resign. This is the surest way."

"Anything particular in mind?"

"It's your assignment, Darius. Whatever you do is all right with me."

"That poor guy treated me like his father-image before. Well—"

"You're not weakening, are you, Darius? There's no time for emotion in this business, none at all. You've got to go out and get a story before some other outfit changes it on you. Or you've got to make *their* stories fail to happen. And whatever you do, you've got to keep the TV outfits guessing. If news starts happening according to Hoyle, we're all through. Us and the *World* and all the other newspapers wouldn't stand a chance, not with TV right on the spot. Keep TV guessing. Confused. Never sure. Give some crumbs to the *World*, even—if you have to.

"So there's no time for thalamic responses, Darius. Do I make myself clear?"

McLeod bristled. "You never had to give me that kind of lecture. You think I'm a cub or something? Don't worry about Mayor Spurgess, we'll fix him up."

"Splendid. But there's something else…Crippens."

"I told you how I felt about that. I don't want any part of it. Talk about your Judas's—"

"Crippens or you, Darius. The *World's* gunning. You know it."

"I can't tell you what to do. But I'll warn Cripp, that's all."

"That would make your own assignment rather difficult."

"What assignment are you talking about?"

"Crippens. The way I figure it, you have a lot at stake there. We'll let you handle Crippens."

"You're crazy!"

"You are if you refuse. We won't give you a single Security man for protection. Remember what they said in COMING EVENTS. Your one chance is to get Crippens before they get you and then let the *World* scoop us. I would

11

suggest the first thing next Monday morning, but then, it's your baby."

"First Mayor Spurgess and now Crippens. Are you trying to make me a hatchetman?"

"A reporter, Darius. You've always been a good one."

"But Crippens is my friend."

"I wish we had another way out. Crippens has his place on the *Star-Times*, but we thought too much of him. We don't want to lose you, Darius. You can take that as an objective compliment and sleep easy. Your job's secure."

"Thank you very much."

"Don't be bitter. A man in the newspaper business is top dog these days, see? I don't have to tell you. We're not passive receptors. We control things. We make things happen. We play God, but we've got competition. You've got to take the good with the bad, that's all. See what I mean?"

All the while they had spoken, Overman had not moved from where he had perched his small frame on his desk, but his nervous legs had walked miles, his scrawny, sleeve-rolled arms had waved, flapped and gesticulated, his wide, bulging eyes had darted about the frenzied confusion of the great room where news was created and missed nothing. It was Overman's passion, McLeod knew, his alpha through omega. He suddenly wished it were that simple for himself. Less than half an hour ago, it would have been.

"We'll have our obituary people compose something tender for Crippens," Overman said. "Keep me informed, Darius."

"I haven't told you I'd do it."

"Whose obit would you rather see them write?"

"You could protect me instead."

But Overman jerked his head side to side again. "It's the same as politics. Much simpler to make news than to prevent it. The one sure way to protect you, provided you don't foul things up with Crippens."

"Well, I don't—"

"One of you makes the obituary page next week. The *World's* already seen to that. Take your choice, Darius."

"Yeah...sure."

"And don't forget about Mayor Spurgess. You've got a busy time ahead of you. Good luck."

Walking back toward his own office, McLeod saw that the flow of co-respondents had slowed to a trickle. He swore softly. The last girl in line was Tracy Kent, a tawny-haired divorce specialist with an admirable record. McLeod liked Tracy, but it was strictly brother-sister stuff.

Tracy was going to marry Harry Crippens.

CHAPTER TWO

"HEY, Darius. A girl gets hungry for lunch around this time every day."

McLeod smiled. "Won't Cripp be along soon?"

"Search me." Tracy started rubbing her stomach under the smooth, tautly drawn fabric of her dress. "When this piece of machinery starts to gurgle, I eat."

"Well, I was going to head over to the Press Club in a few minutes anyway. Don't you have to get yourself caught with someone today?"

"Later on. Tonight. Now I'm hungry."

Tracy Kent was long and almost lean with hips angular rather than rounded. The clean lines of her long-striding legs were accentuated by the tight sheath of skirt as she walked with McLeod toward the elevator. She was all woman unless you happened to look at her a certain way, when you caught a glimpse of something coltish, almost like Peter Pan, in the way she carried herself or smiled at you. She did not look like a vamp, thought McLeod, which helped explain why she was such a successful co-respondent.

"One of these days I'm going to stop feeling like a brother toward you," McLeod promised as they climbed into his copter on the roof.

"You're flattering but tardy, Mr. McLeod. I'm going to marry the guy."

"Crippens?"

"Don't look at me that way. He's your friend, too." Tracy grinned as the rotors flashed above them, then pouted. "Darius, do we have to go to the Press Club for lunch?"

"Mixing business with pleasure, I guess. Got to see some people. Why? Does someone bother you over there?"

"That Weaver Wainwright, always staring at me like he wants to sit down at his thinkwriter and let the world know what it's like with a correspondent. Me."

"Wainwright's one of the men I want to see."

"The *Star-Times'* hot-shot reporter hob-nobbing with that riff-raff from the *World?*"

"You named it," Darius McLeod said as their copter rose up from the roof of the *Star-Times* building and retreated from the checkerboard pattern of other copters resting on their landing squares. "Why the sour face?"

"Because I read COMING EVENTS, Darius. Do you think Wainwright's been assigned the job?"

"It's a damned good guess. He just got back from overseas. He's been sopping up spirits like a blotter over at the club and making nasty noises while waiting for a new job. This is probably his baby."

"Why, Darius?"

"Because he's their number one boy."

"No. I mean, why you?"

McLeod shrugged. "Does there have to be a reason? It's good copy for them. The *Star-Times* loses a guy who's been around, too. That's the newspaper business, Tracy. Don't look for any reason."

"Don't be so calm about it. What's Overman going to do?"

McLeod considered the question as he brought the copter down expertly through the lanes of local traffic here at the edge of the city. Off in the distance, rank on rank of hemispherical suburban homes marched off, in orderly rows, to the eastern horizon. The Press Club, almost directly below them now, had snipped half a dozen square miles from the patterned picture. It was castle, game preserve, and sylvan retreat not for one monarch, but for hundreds. Newshounds, newshens, gunmen. Flashing letters swam up at them from the green woodland, blinking on and off garishly—THE FOURTH ESTATE.

If he told her Overman had failed to offer any protection, she'd realize another alternative had been selected. It would be better if he lied. "What's Overman going to do?" he repeated her question. "The usual. I'll be protected. Don't worry about me."

"But if Wainwright's all they say, he's like a bloodhound. Be careful, Darius."

"Hell, I said don't worry. I have till next week, anyway."

"This is Friday."

"Yeah, Friday." Their copter alighted with hardly a quiver. Uniformed lackies were already polishing the chrome and glass by the time McLeod helped Tracy to the ground. She came down lithely, long hair whipping about her face and brushing against McLeod's cheek. A girl scantily clad as a bathing beauty contestant led them across the landing field and along a path through the gnarled oaks that made the Fourth Estate resemble more a chunk of Scotland than Long Island. But while they couldn't see the acres of neon tubing from the ground, their pulsing glow spoiled the effect.

THE clubhouse itself was an architectural nightmare of quarry-stone, turrets, battlements—and great, soft-hued thermo-glass walls. Music stirred the air faintly with rhythm as they crossed the drawbridge (which actually worked, McLeod knew) and entered the lobby. The pretty little scantily-clad girl disappeared and was replaced at once by the weapon-check girl, dressed in top hat and tails, but not much else.

She smiled professionally at Tracy, then frisked her expertly, finding the trick pocket in her skirt and removing the tiny but deadly parabeam from her leg holster. Tracy grinned back like a yawning cat. "I'd have given it to you."

"I'm sorry, m'am. They all say that." The weaponcheck girl turned to McLeod. "It's the law around here, you know that. Well good afternoon there, Mr. McLeod."

The hands darted with quick, practiced precision over him after he nodded. He felt the sleeve-holster slip out by way of his armpit, was given a numbered check for both weapons as the girl hip-wagged away and suspended their weapons from hooks in her arsenal. They were then led to a table near the bandstand, where they ordered cocktails.

"It's an awful lot of fuss just to eat lunch," Tracy said. "Every time that weapon hen paws me like that, I want to scratch her big, wide eyes out. Darius, I'm still afraid for you. Is Wainwright here?"

"I haven't looked, but don't worry. I have till next week, anyway."

"They could kidnap you and hold you somewhere till they're ready to kill you."

McLeod tried to hide his momentary confusion by making a production of lighting his cigarette and smiling at someone he hardly knew at a nearby table. Tracy certainly had a good point—which he hadn't considered until now.

Tracy glanced about uneasily in the dim light. "Did Overman think of that? I don't see any Security men around."

McLeod exhaled a long plume of smoke and watched it get sucked into the unseen currents of the climatizer. "They don't let themselves get seen," he said easily. "They wouldn't be good Security men if they did, would they?"

"But what are you going to do, Darius? Can't you take some kind of positive action? It's not like you, just sitting around and waiting."

McLeod wanted to change the subject, for Tracy had a way of ferreting out the truth even if she suspected nothing. He'd always thought she was wasting her time as a co-respondent and often told her so, but she'd always countered by striking a bump-and-grind pose and saying she had all the equipment. "Have you heard about Cripp?" he asked her now.

"Only that he was going out on an assignment. Suicide I think."

"Unfortunately, the guy had a change of heart. They had to tear up the obit."

"Was it Cripp's fault?"

"I doubt it. Suicide and murder are two different things. Psychology fouled up, that's all."

"But Overman must have been furious, anyway. Poor Cripp."

"Overman'll get over it," McLeod shot back. "Cripp's a good man."

Tracy shook her head slowly. "Thanks for saying it, but Cripp isn't cut out for the newspaper racket and you know it. A couple more flubs and Overman will begin to think Cripp belongs to the Anti-Newspaper League or something."

"Very funny," McLeod told her. "I can just see it now: Cripp a subversive."

"Shhh!" said Tracy, raising a finger to her lips. "We shouldn't even talk about things like that. Mentioning the Anti-Newspaper League in here is like eating beef-steak in Delhi."

A figure approached their table and sat down at the empty chair without receiving an invitation. "Did I hear something about the Anti-Newspaper League?" the man demanded, chuckling softly. He was tall and gaunt but well-tanned, the whites of his eyes very bright against the skin of his face. He had a long, sad nose, which drooped mournfully almost to his upper lip, mitigating the effect of his smile.

He was Weaver Wainwright, ace reporter of the *World*.

"WERE just a couple of subversives, Mr. Wainwright," Tracy said.

"So that's why the *Star-Times* is filling its pages with wrongos these days. How do you do, McLeod?"

"Never felt better. Ought to live to be a hundred, at least. Can we get you something?"

"As a matter of fact, I've just had lunch. Brandy might help my sluggish liver, though."

"Brandy it is," said McLeod, and gave the new order to their waiter when he arrived with a pair of Gibsons. "According to what I read in the papers, the *World's* thinking of starting a Tong War with us." McLeod hid his impulse to smile by making a conventional toast to Tracy. He wondered how much his unexpected candor had unnerved Wainwright and decided to study the reporter's reaction carefully.

But Wainwright merely grinned, making the upper lip all but disappear and the nose become more prominent. "At least you read a good newspaper," he said. "I don't think it's fair for you to say we had war in mind, McLeod. Nothing of the sort. Our Prognostication division merely indicated that a certain well-known opposition newsman was going to meet with an unfortunate accident next week. And while prognostication is pretty reliable—especially coming from a good newspaper—it's hardly the last word. Ah…here's my brandy." And he began to sip and stare over the rim of his glass at Tracy.

"Nice stay in Europe?" McLeod wanted to know. Under the circumstances, Wainwright's composure had been admirable.

"Fair. But then, you read the papers."

"You mean that business about Yugoslavia and France?"

"That's right. Your man—what's his name, Kitrick?—thought there would be peace. He's wrong, you know. All you have to do is touch a spark to the right fuse in the Balkans I always said. Kitrick was trying to put the fire out by spitting."

"Wayne Kitrick didn't think there was any fire to put out," Tracy told the *World* reporter. "As of now, there isn't."

"Give it some time," Wainwright promised. "You see, the President of Yugoslavia was indiscreet in his youth, most indiscreet. With elections approaching there, he had the alternative of—well, you know what a newspaper can do to a man of position who's been indiscreet. Drink to it?"

They did. In spite of everything, McLeod had to admire Wainwright. Back in the old days, nations went to war for economic reasons, over diametrically opposed political philosophies, because of religion. Today, a sharp reporter dug deep to unearth closeted skeletons and moral potsherds and literally blackmailed a chief of state into war. Wainwright was sharp all right. History might one day write up the whole series of twenty-second century wars as "Blackmail Wars," but meanwhile the U. N. could only gnash it's collective teeth while Wainwright picked up a fattened paycheck.

"I'll bet you're proud of yourself," Tracy said.

"I don't see why not. Kitrick will be reamed, my dear."

"And so will a few million innocent people."

"Perhaps you weren't fooling when you mentioned the Anti-Newspaper League. But of course, you're pulling my leg."

"I'm a co-respondent," Tracy said coldly. "I don't have to turn cart wheels over your end of the newspaper game."

"Tracy," McLeod said. This was one facet of the girl's character he'd never seen before. He could almost see the gears meshing into place inside Wainwright's skull. He didn't mind talk that bordered on the subversive, as long as it came from Tracy, who was quite outspoken about a lot of things, but Wainwright might have other ideas.

But Wainwright said, blandly, "From a moral standpoint you carve out your pound of flesh every now and then too, my dear. Or don't you think framing innocent men in compromising circumstances is immoral?"

"You wouldn't understand the difference," Tracy said.

"It is a difference of degree, not kind."

TRACY bit her lips and did not reply. It was like a revelation to McLeod. He suddenly wondered if Cripp knew how maladjusted his fiancée was.

Abruptly, Wainwright changed the subject. "Are you well insured, McLeod?"

"I never could figure out who to name as beneficiary."

"That's a shame."

"If you've planned anything now, I thought you'd like to know *Star-Times* Security Forces are all around us," McLeod bluffed.

"You underestimate me, sir. Prognostication comes up with the raw facts, which I sift for story material. I merely wait for things to happen. However, in case you have any inclinations to put the shoe on the other foot, I'm sure you realize *World* Security men often lunch at the Fourth Estate."

That, McLeod suspected, was no bluff. Tracy was still nibbling on her lip but managed to cast a worried look in his direction. They ordered and ate in silence while Wainwright swirled and sipped another brandy.

"Have you heard about poor Mayor Spurgess?" Wainwright asked as McLeod cooled his coffee with cream.

McLeod scalded his lips. The *World* reporter was playing cat-and-mouse with him, taunting him overtly. Perhaps Wainwright figured he could kill two birds with one stone, getting McLeod while McLeod tried to protect the mayor's record. He hoped Wainwright had not thought of Overman's alternative.

"You're a busy man," McLeod finally said.

"I detest inactivity. I assume since you wrote Mayor Spurgess into office, you are going to protect his name. Miss Kent, could you excuse yourself for a moment?"

Tracy waited until McLeod nodded, then stood up and mumbled something about going to powder her nose. McLeod lit a cigarette and waited.

"Now we can talk," Wainwright said. "Recognize the spirit in which this is said, McLeod: you're a fine reporter."

"Thanks."

"But you're as good as dead. We've written your obituary."

Strangely, the announcement brought no fear. Although it had only been a couple of hours, McLeod felt as if he'd been living with the idea for years. "You haven't printed it yet."

"In time. But we don't have to print it. Naturally, it's news, McLeod. You have a well-known name. But there are others equally well known. More well known. We can come up with a wrongo occasionally. Basically, we want to kill you because you're too valuable to the *Star-Times.*"

"Your motive doesn't interest me. And I have some news for you: I'm a long way from dead."

"Don't be melodramatic, McLeod. We'll get you. A routine assassination-accident doesn't often become a wrongo, you know that. We have decided to make an offer to you."

Now McLeod's skin did begin to crawl. Statistically, the assassination-accident case was more foolproof than any other. Gunmen commanded good salaries and did their work expertly. Ninety-five per cent accuracy could be expected. "I'm listening."

"Join the *World.*"

"Come again?"

"I'm sure you heard me. Quit the *Star-Times* and join us. We'll match your salary, we won't kill you—"

"But the *Star-Times will!*"

"You'd be valuable to us, aside from your abilities as a reporter. No doubt, they've included you in any long-range plans they might have. We'll have them piling up wrongos from now till doomsday."

"Which is exactly why they'll have me killed if I become a turn-coat."

"We'll offer you full protection."

"I'm already getting full protection—from the *Star-Times*," McLeod lied. It was almost a tempting offer, although it's virtues were purely negative. The *Star-Times* had refused to offer him protection because Overman thought it would be simpler and more certain to serve up a substitute reporter for the kill. If McLeod accepted Wainwright's offer, at least he'd be able to sleep easy regarding Crippens. But if the *World's* real purpose was to remove McLeod from the *Star-Times'* staff, one way or the other, they might risk an all-out Tong War and still gun for him.

Besides, no turncoat newspaperman had ever survived six months. McLeod knew it and was sure Wainwright knew it and guessed the *World* reporter was promising him all he could under the circumstances—a temporary reprieve.

"I know what you're thinking," Wainwright told him. "The *Star-Times* will get you if you turn on them. If necessary, they'll drop everything else until you're dead."

"Well, yes. That's just what I was thinking."

"I don't envy your position," Wainwright admitted. "You believe I'm offering you a few months more of life at best. But you're mistaken, McLeod. *It will appear as if we have killed you.* We can do it, working together. But I offer you life. The accident will all but destroy you, although means of identification will remain. Don't you see what I'm driving at? We can substitute some derelict for you, then change your appearance and employ you on the *World*. The *Star-Times* will never know the difference."

IT was a daring plan. It was just the sort of thing that made the newspaper business in general—and Weaver Wainwright in particular—so omnipotent these days. McLeod did not try to hide his interest. The plan had more than negative virtues after all.

"How do I know I can trust you?" McLeod asked.

"I'm afraid you don't. But let it simmer. What it boils down to is this: you're going to have to take a calculated risk either way, McLeod. No doubt, you've devised some scheme to give us a fat wrongo instead of your corpse. It may or may not work. Statistics say it will not. On the other hand, I promise you life. My plan not only could work, it *should* work. The risk there is that I may not be telling the truth. You'll have to decide...here comes Miss Kent."

"The girl with the crooked face," said Tracy, sitting down. "Unless you tell me it's straight."

"As an arrow," said McLeod, hardly hearing his own words. The more he thought of Wainwright's plan, the better he liked it. If Wainwright were telling the truth, he'd be able to get both Cripp and himself off the hook at the same time. "I'll think about it," he told the *World* reporter, who was smiling and getting up to leave.

"Call me," Wainwright said, and was gone.

"What did he want?" Tracy asked.

"The usual," McLeod told her, realizing a near-truth was often the best lie. "That I join up with the *World* and get protected."

"You wouldn't last a month and you know it. So why did you tell him you'd think about it?"

"To let him think I was playing both ends against dead center, I guess. I don't know. I just want to come out of this thing alive, Tracy."

"I was thinking. There must be something we could dig up about Weaver Wainwright, something we could hold over his head so he'd rather be guilty of a wrongo than see it revealed."

"I doubt it. Anyway, you don't blackmail newspapermen."

"You don't kill them, either. Darius, did you ever stop to think how—how awfully evil this whole setup is? I don't mean just about you and how the *World* wants to make a story out of killing off the opposition. I mean everything. I mean Weaver Wainwright starting a war in Europe so his paper can get the inside story on it. I mean the President of Yugoslavia being blackmailed by a simple garden-variety newspaperman. I mean Cripp getting chewed out because he went to cover a suicide and the man didn't jump. We ought to celebrate, don't you see? A human life was saved. I mean me getting myself caught with important men so their wives sue for divorce and we get the story. I mean disease that doesn't have to happen and medical cures held back until one paper or another can scoop them. I mean scientific discoveries that aren't made because research scientists and development engineers are on newspaper payrolls and perform their basic research and experiments, then wait for the newspaper stories to be released at an editor's leisure. I mean…oh, what's the use? You're laughing at me."

McLeod was trying not to smile but meeting with little success. "I just never heard you talk like that before, that's all. Tracy, you're like a little girl in a lot of ways—idealistic, romantic, building castles on air and not accepting the real world, but—"

"Real!" Tracy cried. "It's phony from the word go. We're making it that way—to suit headlines."

"Stop shouting," McLeod said in alarm. "People are staring at you."

"I don't care about them."

"Well, I do. Before you know it, they'll be investigating you for Anti-Newspaper tendencies. What's the matter with you?"

"Good lord! Don't sound so gosh-awful righteous, Darius. You treat this newspaper business like a religion."

"Maybe I like being top dog."

"So now you're going to get yourself killed. A sacrifice to the Headline God."

"Stop it," McLeod said. "I won't get killed if I can help it."

"And if Wainwright can help it too, is that the idea?"

"What are you talking about?"

"Sometimes I...I hate you, Darius McLeod. That's what I'm talking about. They're going to kill someone else and change your face and let you work for the *World.*" Tracy stood up and patted her lips with a napkin.

McLeod climbed to his feet too. "How did you know about that?"

"Don't bother getting up. I can find my way back alone, thank you."

McLeod sat down, staring at her.

"Maybe it's because I'm a spy. Maybe I work for the *World.*" Tracy pivoted and stalked away, her heels click clacking defiantly on the marble floor. McLeod gaped after her until she disappeared.

CHAPTER THREE

McCLEOD made an appointment to see Jack Lantrel, the Gunman Chief of the *Star-Times,* Saturday morning. He spent the remainder of Friday pondering and drinking a little too much. The combination yielded a hangover, but not even tentative conclusions. While Tracy Kent had become an unexpected enigma, he couldn't spend too much time on it. Wainwright's proposal nagged at all his thoughts, but he kept telling himself he couldn't trust the *World* reporter. And for the first time he found he didn't like the feeling of power inherent in a newspaperman's position. Having the power of life and death over nameless, faceless people was one thing, but playing the role of the Greek hag who snipped the thread of life with a pair of indifferent scissors for Crippens was quite another.

Lantrel met McLeod in the Gunman's office, greeted him and said, "Dragging me down on Saturday, this better be important." Jack Lantrel was a harried-looking little man. You always expected a great, bosomy wife to come charging in to henpeck him, although, like McLeod, Lantrel was a bachelor. He straightened the thinkwriter and the other items of office equipment on his desk with mechanical efficiency. He was an old fuddy-duddy, thought McLeod, but he had signed the death warrants for hundreds of people.

"It's a job," said McLeod.

"Well, that's what I draw my check for. But we work on a rigid schedule, Darius."

"Then call it a priority job. Mayor Spurgess."

Lantrel looked up from where he'd been drumming his fingers idly on the desk. "Motive is none of my business," he admitted. "But did you say you want to have Mayor Spurgess gunned?"

McLeod sighed. "Yeah…"

"I'm glad my particular job is comparatively simple. You just elected the guy."

"And now we want him killed. Overman would sleep easier and so would I if you did it by tomorrow night."

Lantrel grunted something, prodded the intercom button on his desk and demanded in his high-pitched voice, "Will you please get me the habit file on Mayor Spurgess?" He turned to McLeod. "Sunday night, eh? That doesn't give us much time."

McLeod shrugged and watched a secretary bring in a bulging plastic file envelope, which Lantrel flipped through expertly. "Here we are. Subject generally dines late Sunday night, reviews his Monday morning schedule, smokes a pipe and plays with the TV set until he's convinced there's nothing to interest him, then…oh! Here we are…takes a walk around twenty-two hundred hours, alone, without his wife."

"Sounds simple," McLeod said.

"An assassination-accident," Lantrel informed him with surprising enthusiasm, "is never simple. Despite the statistical expectancy of success, there are too many random factors you have to contend with. If the weather's bad, perhaps the subject won't take his evening constitutional. Perhaps subject's wife will break the pattern with some company for dinner. Subject might conceivably take a friend along with him. You see what I'm driving at?"

McLeod nodded. "All I want to know is this: can you do the job Sunday night?"

Lantrel scanned the file again. "Subject leaves his house at twenty-two hundred, returns by twenty-two forty-five. That gives us forty-five minutes. Probably, Darius."

"Good enough."

LANTREL slid a gunman form into his thinkwriter, hunched himself down in his chair and watched the machine type. Presently the sheet of paper slipped out the other side of the squat machine and McLeod read:

DATE: 14 Dec 2103
NAME: Darius John McLeod
ASSIGNMENT (CURRENT): City Desk
JOB NO.: 03-4-12
CLASSIFICATION: Top Priority
SUBJECT: Peter Winston Spurgess. Mayor, New York City
DATE OF EXECUTION (APPROX): 15 Dec 2103
METHOD: Vehicular, or other, accident
CODE: 4-12-DJM
APPROVED: /s/Jack Lantrel

JACK LANTREL
GUNMAN EDITOR

THE UNDERSIGNED HEREBY CERTIFIES THAT JOB NO. 03-4-12, HEREAFTER REFERRED TO AS 4-12-DJM, HAS BEEN ORDERED IN COMPLIANCE WITH THE EXISTING REGULATIONS GOVERNING ASSASSINATION-ACCIDENTS, AND THAT 4-12-DJM HAS BEEN APPROVED, ORALLY OR IN WRITING, BY THE City Editor. THE UNDERSIGNED IS COGNIZANT OF THE FACT THAT ANY FRAUD OR DECEIT IN THIS APPLICATION, WHETHER FOR PERSONAL GAIN OR OTHERWISE, IS PUNISHABLE BY SUMMARY REVOCATION OF HIS (HER) NEWSPAPER LICENSE.

DARIUS JOHN McLEOD

It suddenly was no simple matter for McLeod to scrawl his name at the bottom of the sheet. He was aware of Lantrel, a puzzled expression on his face, watching him. It seemed entirely routine to affix his signature, but quite suddenly he was aware of the machinery that would put into operation. Gunmen would be selected for the job, would study Mayor Spurgess' habit file, would agree with Lantrel on the *modus operandi*. Within thirty-six hours, Mayor Spurgess would be dead.

Darius McLeod executioner?

Hardly. He was merely carrying out an assignment. Newspapers were active agents in the modern world. If it had not been his assignment, it would have been someone else's. You could hardly consider it murder. Murder was punishable today as it had always been—by capital punishment or a long prison term. A newspaperman was above reproach—or imprisonment.

McLeod saw the parallel that he had first seen in Overman's office yesterday. He was both executioner and victim. Even now as he was signing the application for Mayor Spurgess' death, perhaps Weaver Wainwright was signing one that read, SUBJECT: Darius John McLeod, reporter, New York *Star-Times*. The *World* Gunman Editor might now be studying his habit file, weighing the various factors to determine what situation seemed most promising as a vessel for his "accidental" death. Did the editor know that McLeod often spent weekends racing across country or down to South America in his jet? It was there in his habit file in all probability. Did he know that McLeod visited the *Star-Times* space station once every fortnight because he was being groomed to cover the *Star-Times* dash to the moon, if ever they got the jump on the *World* space station and could leave Earth's gravitational field without the near-certainty of being tracked and shot down by a *World* rocket? Did he know the thousand one little habits which, combined in various predictable patterns, made up McLeod's life? Unfortunately, the answer had to be in the affirmative. It left McLeod feeling a little sick.

"What's the matter, Darius? Is something wrong?"

"Huh? No... Nothing." McLeod signed the application. "There you are."

"Fine," said Lantrel, placing the application in his out basket. "Call me at home tomorrow afternoon, Darius. I'll give you the details so you can cover the assignment. You know the number?"

McLeod said that he did and left. He wondered if Weaver Wainwright would make a similar call. The worst part of it was that he didn't know when.

WHEN he reached his bachelor apartment in the East Seventies, the door recorder told him that two visitors, one male and one female, were waiting for him. McLeod felt the comforting bulk of his parabeam in its arm holster and loosened it there. If they had entered his apartment it was because their fingerprint patterns had been included in the locking mechanism, but he couldn't take any chances. He opened the door and sighed his relief.

"Morning, Darius," Harry Crippens greeted him cheerfully, bouncing up from a web-chair and extending his hand. "Shake hands with a reporter who just got a big, fat, unexpected raise."

McLeod lit a cigarette and said, "I'm very glad to hear that, Cripp. Did Overman tell you?"

"Nope. First I knew of it, I read it in the paper. Take a look."

As McLeod took this morning's *Star-Times* from Crippens, Tracy entered the living room from the kitchen. "Coffee in a minute, Cripp," she said. "Oh, Darius. We're making ourselves to home, as the expression goes. Did you see that crazy thing in the paper?"

"I'm about to," said McLeod.

"Crazy!" Crippens cried in mock horror. "I get a raise right before we get married and she says crazy."

"Well, it doesn't make sense." McLeod turned to the Internal Affairs page of the *Star-Times*. With the newspaper profession supplanting Hollywood fifty-odd years ago as the world's most glamorous, articles on internal affairs had evolved from small islands of type in a sea of advertisements to a place of importance with their own daily page and special editor.

"Three column head," Crippens said proudly. "Liberal quotes from the King himself...Maestro Overman."

"That's what I mean," Tracy repeated. "Crazy. Only yesterday he was chewing you out."

The article said that a new star was on the *Star-Times* horizon, and went on to discuss all the successful assignments Crippens had handled. There was no mention of his wrongos, which McLeod knew were considerable. A two-column cut of Crippens at his thinkwriter was included and the caption rendered a thumbnail biography. The article concluded by mentioning a raise in salary, which gave Crippens more than Tracy and almost what McLeod earned.

"That's great," McLeod said, finding it difficult to maintain his enthusiasm. Damn Overman, he didn't miss a trick. Fattening the calf for slaughter.

"Now the girl's got to marry me," Crippens declared. "I earn more money than she does." He was flip, building effusively in the best newspaperman fashion. He was not the serious, intent Crippens McLeod had always known, although, on closer examination, McLeod realized that the owlish eyes looked quite sober.

"Quit your kidding," McLeod told him. "Harry Crippens would probably celebrate by discussing his next assignment, or making a study of the moral factors involved. What's the matter?"

"Not a thing," Crippens assured him easily. "Here, have a drink. It's your whisky."

"In the morning?" asked Tracy.

"This is a celebration, girl. There you go." And Crippens sloshed liquor into three glasses. His hands were shaking.

"I said what's the matter?" McLeod ignored the drink.

Crippens didn't. "Not a thing. Not a single, solitary thing."

"Go ahead and talk to him," Tracy said.

"Don't mind her, Darius. Have another?" Crippens poured for himself.

"Darn it, Cripp. Even if it means making me feel better?"

"Darius wouldn't do a thing like that, that's all."

"Like what?" McLeod wanted to know.

"I have to hand it to you," Tracy told him. "I thought you'd do your best to change the subject."

"Like nothing," Crippens said. "I mean it, don't mind her. She had some silly idea…I don't even want to talk about it."

"Darius," Tracy asked abruptly, "what have you decided to do about Weaver Wainwright?"

"Please," said Crippens.

"I haven't made up my mind yet. I'm not going to let him kill me if I can help it."

"Do tell. Does Cripp fit into the picture at all?"

McLeod hoped he could substitute evasion for outright lying. "Why don't you ask Overman?"

"Because I'm asking you."

He didn't think Tracy would ask Overman. He didn't think Overman would tell her the truth if she did. He saw she was waiting for an answer and said, "If the answer to that question were yes, you wouldn't expect me to tell you. If it were no, I ought to consider it an insult, coming from friends."

"We never stood on ceremonies before, Darius."

"Tracy, for gosh sakes!" Crippens pleaded. "Darius is my friend."

"I'm still waiting for an answer."

McLeod walked to the door and opened it. Crippens opened his mouth to speak, but changed his mind. He glared at Tracy.

"Get out of here," McLeod said. He was behaving like a child he realized. But more than anything else, he needed time to think.

Tracy went through the doorway, staring straight ahead. McLeod wished she would look at him, or holler, or slap him. She said, "All right, Darius. If that's the way you want to play it."

McLeod heard them arguing in low tones as he shut the door behind them.

Just what do you do, he thought, when your whole world starts to blow up all around you? You don't kick over the remaining traces. You try to re-establish the familiar, comforting pattern in some small way.

McLeod called the mayor's residence and got through to Spurgess at once. The flabby, thick-jowled face looked sickly white, like putty.

"McLeod, thank God. I thought you'd forgotten."

"Not on your life. I just wanted to tell you everything's going to be fine. You won't have to resign your office for political corruption. We'll see to that."

"Oh, thank you," said Mayor Spurgess. "Thank you very much."

"Sure," said McLeod, and cut the connection. Give or take a couple, Mayor Spurgess had about thirty-six hours to live.

And McLeod...?

SNOW was falling in thick, slow flakes, which melted on contact with the ground when McLeod went outside after lunch. Since neither the *Star-Times* nor the *World* was depending on the cold virus or influenza for medical headlines this season, it was comparatively safe venturing out in this weather.

This, McLeod thought, seeing it for the first time in a strange, new light, was the city. Gray-white sky, overflowing snowflakes. Slidewalks, covered for the winter, conducting crowds of bovinely unaware people from place to place. Steel and glass and stone, soaring skyward, disappearing in the feathery white snow that, up above, was not feathery at all but a solid gray pall.

Did the cud-munching people know the truth about newspapers? McLeod doubted it. The old name had remained—newspapers—but the function had changed. We give them each day their daily cud. We don't report. We motivate. You didn't find it anyplace. It wasn't written. It happened and it was accepted. Maybe they did know. It might make a good book, if people ever went back to reading books again; Not yellow journalism, but ROY G. BIV journalism, for all the colors in the rainbow. Concepts had changed. How? After the Third World War? The Fourth? People wanted to believe what they read. Each individual existence was precarious, cliff-edged, ready to fall or scramble back to safety. People believed. Almost, it was as if they had forgotten their Western Christian heritage, in which they moved through time from past to future, active agents in a static environment. Now they embodied the old Greek idea.

People didn't flow. Time did. They stood backwards in the river of time, with the future flowing up, unseen, behind them, becoming the present, flowing on and becoming the past, which lay, decipherable, before their eyes. Only newspapermen had eyes in the back of their heads.

Look out! Cancer's coming. I read it in the *World*. (The World Medical Corps sows the seed, and the incidence of cancer increases.) Good newspaper, the *World*. Always lets you know what's coming. I see where the *Star-Times* says the cancer rate is dropping. Hope they're right. (Newspaper Medical Corps battle mightily, offstage, and the *Star-Times* wins. Temporarily, no more cancer.) What do you know, the *Star-Times* was right.

Star-Times says we ought to have a spaceship on the moon soon. Thrilling, isn't it (*Star-Times* astronauts prepare to launch a two-stage rocket from their space station, but *World* astronauts intercept it with a guided missile and destroy it.) Well, looks like the *World* was right. Space travel soon, but not yet.

Senator Blundy's daughter was attacked on the campus of that there college up state, what's its name? You read about it in the *Star-Times*? You know, it's not so bad, being small time, I always say. Things like that only happen to important people. Yes sir, we're lucky.

World says it's a Brinks, one of those unsolved robberies. Three million dollars from the Bank of New York! (But *Star-Times* detectives go to work and find—or sometimes frame— the criminal.) Hey, it's not a Brinks anymore. Maybe I ought to read the *Star-Times* more often.

That Weaver Wainwright earns six hundred thousand dollars a year, but my kid wants to be a politician. Some kids you just can't figure.

McLeod wandered into a bar and got himself mellowed, then found another and repeated the process. When he returned to the street and made his way to the sidewalk, the snow had finally begun to stick. Someone in the bar had recognized him and asked for an autograph. It hadn't stirred him at all. Was he maturing or turning sour?

Returning home as dusk descended on the city and streetlights gleamed on three inches of snow, McLeod learned from his door recorder that he had one female visitor. That would be Tracy, he thought, and prepared himself for more unpleasantness. Why couldn't they leave him alone?

"Come in, Darius. Shut the door." He did both, turned, and saw Tracy pointing a parabeam at him. His hand fumbled with the trick sleeve of his jacket, but the storm-coat got in his way. Tracy's parabeam zipped audibly and McLeod turned to stone.

CHAPTER FOUR

"I'LL unfreeze your head so you can talk. You realize I ought to kill you."

His head tingled and he found that he could open his mouth, blink his eyes and twitch his nose. He couldn't turn his neck. From the chin down he was helplessly immobile. He was a disembodied brain with a face. He wished he were sober.

"Cripp still doesn't believe me," Tracy said. "He insisted I come back alone and apologize. So I came back."

"But not to apologize."

"To get some information, Darius. I could be wrong. I don't think I am."

"Out at the Fourth Estate yesterday, you knew what kind of proposition Wainwright had made me," McLeod said, stalling for time while he tried to summon a logical defense. His mind was almost a blank.

"Sometimes I talk too much. Yes, I knew. Never mind how. I'm doing the questioning, and I want answers. When I read about Cripp in the Internal Affairs section, I put two and two together. Wainwright's assignment had been vague, so I guessed you and Overman had decided some substitution might be in order."

McLeod was silent.

"I advise you to talk, Darius. If I killed you now, it would be a bit ahead of schedule, but I think that would still satisfy Wainwright. Don't you?"

"You're bluffing," McLeod said—and hoped. "You couldn't possibly be on assignment to kill me. So you'd be subject to the same laws which face the general public for murder."

"All right. Maybe I won't kill you. But you feel no pain under a parabeam, Darius. Remember that. I could start burning your hand with my lighter and work up to your elbow and you wouldn't even know—until I unfroze you."

"You wouldn't," McLeod said. "Maybe we don't see eye to eye now, but we're friends."

Tracy began nibbling at her lip. Her eyes were big and watery, as if she'd been fighting back tears. "Sure—I liked you. Maybe I still do. I don't know. I'm all mixed up. You know me, Darius. I'm liable to do anything—*anything*—when I'm all mixed up like this. I don't want to hurt you, not if I can help it. I like you, Darius. We've had fun together. Great times."

"That's better." McLeod's confidence was returning. He'd be out of freeze in no time now. "Just unfreeze me, and we can talk about this like two sensible people."

"I like you, but I'm in love with Cripp." Tracy removed her lighter from a pocket of her blouse with trembling fingers. She lit a cigarette and didn't extinguish the flame. She came closer to McLeod.

"Cut it out," he said. He felt sweat rolling down his forehead from his hairline and making his eyes blink. Parabeaming did peculiar, unpredictable things to the metabolism. The room seemed furnace-hot.

"Then answer my question."

There was no sense being maimed, McLeod finally decided. Tracy knew the truth anyway. She just wanted to hear him say it. But now she brought a tiny mini-recorder into view from where it had been resting on a table and flipped the switch to on.

"What's that for?"

"Cripp. I want him to know. I want him to be able to protect himself from you. We're recording now, Darius. Answer this question—do you and Overman plan to use Cripp as a substitute corpse to satisfy Weaver Wainwright and the *World?* Is that why Cripp got his raise and all that unexpected publicity?"

McLeod licked his lips and tried to look down as Tracy's hand disappeared from view with the lighter. He saw no smoke but imagined his flesh beginning to crisp.

"Answer me. Did you and Overman plan to kill Cripp and give Wainwright his story that way?"

McLeod read nothing in her eyes, not even hatred. He said, "Yes. That's right."

Tracy shut off the mini-recorder, pocketed her lighter. She reversed the parabeam and McLeod felt his limbs begin to tingle with minute sparks of pain.

"Don't try anything," Tracy said. "I'm still pointing this at you." Her voice caught. She tried to speak again but sobbed.

McLeod brought his arm up slowly and examined it. No damage.

"I—I guess you know I couldn't do it, Darius. I couldn't hurt you. But I don't want you to hurt Cripp. I want to give Cripp a fair chance. Have you signed an application for his death yet?"

"No."

"Will you?"

They were friends again. McLeod couldn't sense it. Friends who might try to hurt each other, of necessity, but friends. "I don't know," he said.

"Give him a break, Darius. There must be another way out. I could tell you things, if I could only trust you..."

McLeod laughed easily, massaging his forearms. "Better not," he said. "Better get out of here."

"Maybe someday."

"Maybe. Thanks for telling me you couldn't do it. That's good to know." He shouldn't have said that. He was acting compulsively, striking back blindly.

The color left Tracy's face. "That was only because you haven't actually threatened Cripp yet. Don't rely on it, though."

She was striking back, too. He staggered to the door and watched her go. Crippens had himself a good woman there, the lucky s.o.b. Maybe that was why he hadn't rejected the idea of killing Crippens, McLeod thought.

SLEEPING that night, after a dinner that felt like slag inside him, McLeod dreamed he had just signed an application for his own demise on the steps of City Hall while bands played and people cheered. Mayor Spurgess was there with a television camera and kept on pleading for McLeod not to renege, but Tracy clung to the mayor's arm and tried to lure him away to a co-respondent rendezvous. Weaver Wainwright and Overman lurked on the fringe of the crowd, both pointing at McLeod and laughing. Harry Crippens was the gunman.

When McLeod awoke, a gray dawn was seeping in through the windows. He showered and downed some bicarbonate of soda in water, but still felt like hell. A mantle of snow covered the silent streets outside and more snow was falling. Even the meteorologist's job wasn't guesswork now, McLeod thought wryly. Predicting snow, the *Star-Times* had sowed the clouds for it.

It was suddenly very important for Mayor Spurgess not to die.

Early in the afternoon, McLeod called Jack Lantrel at home, but a pert-faced girl smiled at him from the screen. "I'm sorry, Mr. Lantrel is not at home. Is there a message?"

"It's important that I reach him," McLeod said.

41

"Mr. Lantrel is out. He left no number. What is it in reference to?"

"4-12-DJM," McLeod said, and waited while the receptionist disappeared from view.

"You're Mr. McLeod, aren't you?"

"That's right."

"You don't have to worry about 4-12-DJM, sir. Everything will be taken care of."

"There's been a change of plans. I want the gunmen called off."

The professional smile was replaced by a frown. "Only Mr. Lantrel can do that."

"That's why I want to reach him. I told you it was important."

"But I don't know when he'll be back. Confidentially, sir, Mr. Lantrel just hates snow. When he read in the paper it was going to snow, he said he was leaving town. I'm sorry."

McLeod asked if she knew where Lantrel usually went.

"That's hard to say. He likes to forget about business, you see. He's down south," she added brightly. "Someplace down south. Is there any message?"

"Yes," McLeod said. "I'll be home all day. If Mr. Lantrel calls, have him contact me at once."

But as the afternoon dragged on, McLeod thought it unlikely that the Gunman Chief would receive his message. He had reached the unexpected decision about Mayor Spurgess quite suddenly and now found it almost beyond analysis. He neither liked the mayor nor disliked him. It was not the man who must live, but the symbol.

Symbol? Of what?

McLeod found the idea mildly ridiculous, almost as if he were drumming up trade for the Anti-Newspaper League, self-proselytizing. It wasn't that for the first time in his life, he told himself, he found an intrinsic evil in the newspaper business. It was simply that the system had hit home for the first time, unexpectedly. He had set the machinery in motion for Mayor Spurgess' death; Weaver Wainwright had done the same for him; Overman had decided the *Star-Times* could not afford to lose his services but could manage without Harry Crippens.

There was no logical connection. If Mayor Spurgess died, that was that. Flowers and a sad song for the widow. But the whole Wainwright-McLeod-Overman-Crippens problem still remained unsolved. Not to mention Tracy Kent.

Had he become anti-newspaper? The term almost defied definition. The Anti-Newspaper League was one thing, formal, organized, purposeful. But anti-newspaper could mean a lot of things. It could mean slight deviation, non-conformity, the simple desire to earn your keep in some other line. Such a desire was never realized, however. There were only three classes of newspapermen: working reporters, corpses, and retired hounds and hens who lived on newspaper farms in old-folk luxury. A newspaperman simply knew too much to be allowed to change his line of work.

No, there was a fourth type. There was the Anti-Newspaper League. What was the old word—Quisling? It referred to politics or some other fields of endeavor, McLeod thought. He wasn't sure what. They were on newspaper payrolls but tried to gum up the works.

Logic was getting him nowhere. He belonged to no cut-and-dry category.

He wanted Mayor Spurgess to live.

Lantrel failed to call by dinnertime or afterwards. At twenty-hundred thirty, McLeod zipped on an insulined jumper, checked his parabeam and went out into the *Star-Times* snow.

CHAPTER FIVE

HIDDEN heat-coils melted the snow that managed to drift over the slidewalks despite their protective canopies, but the streets were covered with snow now more than a foot deep. McLeod felt it crunch underfoot as he left the slidewalks and headed for the mayor's house.

His breath exhaled in quick vapor-puffs against the cold, brittle air. His feet were heavy in the snow but dry. His was the only set of footsteps marring the white blanket that covered everything.

It occurred to him all at once that Mayor Spurgess would likely forego his evening walk because of the weather, which necessitated another type of accident. Lantrel's men were both experienced and imaginative. You could write a book categorizing all the possibilities…

Wind whipped around corners and sprayed McLeod's face with snowflakes. He heard a voice calling far off in the fuzzy white dimness, but soon it was gone. Finally, he reached the mayor's stately house—a redbrick, white-columned Georgian structure, massive and secure on a large corner lot. He crouched behind a leafless privet hedgerow in the driveway and waited, peering up occasionally at the cheery yellow squares of light that were the second storey windows. His ear-crono whispered the time to him: twenty-two hundred hours.

The telltale footsteps he had left in the snow were fast disappearing as the flakes fell thicker. He slid his parabeam out through the jumper's trick sleeve and felt the cold air knifing momentarily into his bare arm. The feeling of warm security, so paradoxical under the circumstances, left him. If he foiled Lantrel's gunmen, Overman would learn of it. If he didn't foil them but tried—which seemed more likely—Overman would also hear.

Just what was he doing here, anyway? He flexed his stiff muscles and was on the point of standing up when he saw three figures approaching down the street, vague as ghosts in the snow. There was still time. He could intercept them and say he had come to cover the story, something that was expected of him. He wondered what sort of accident they had planned.

He jogged toward them through the snow, met them still half a block from Spurgess' house. Two were young, possibly still in training. They were tall and looked like soldiers in their slick jumpers. They stared at him arrogantly. The third was shorter, heavier, of calculating eye. The expression of the first two faces said: *we're gunmen—whatever you are, we're better.* The third face said: *we'd as soon kill you as spit, but we don't kill except for hire or when provoked in the line of duty.*

"I'm from the paper," McLeod told them, whispering. "Here to cover the story."

The three faces stared back at him through the snow, crystalizing what he had felt all day but had not been able to explain.

Those faces...

They had nothing against Mayor Spurgess. Perhaps they had never even seen him. If they didn't like him and had a reason and wanted to kill him, that wouldn't be so bad. That would be fine. But they were here to kill him because McLeod had signed the application along with Lantrel. They wanted to do the job and get back to warmer places and hot buttered rum or whatever they liked.

"He come out yet?" the older gunman asked.

"I don't think he will, not in this weather. What other plans have you got?"

"We'll just wait and see. We don't have to make the plans."

Had they been able to read McLeod's face as readily as he had read theirs? "I don't understand," he said. "You'll have to think of something else if he doesn't take his walk, won't you?"

"You said you were from the paper?"

"Of course."

"Well, you're not making sense."

McLEOD toyed with his parabeam, then watched as matching weapons leaped into the hands of the two younger gunmen.

"Which paper?" the older one drawled.

McLeod felt his heart flutter wildly and checked a strong impulse to laugh.

One of the young gunmen said, "I thought the big boy himself was covering this...Wainwright. I know what he looks like."

"Come on, guy. Which paper?"

McLeod knew the mistake could be fatal. Somehow the *World* had learned what the *Star-Times* had planned for Mayor Spurgess. These men were *World* gunmen, come to thwart Lantrel's men. Perhaps they could, but McLeod might die in the process.

"Listen," he said desperately. "The other day, Weaver Wainwright made me a proposition."

"Who *are* you, guy?"

"Darius McLeod. Hold on, damn it! If you freeze me now, you'll be making a mistake. Wainwright wanted me to work for the *World*. That's why I'm here, don't you understand? I can tell you exactly what the *Star-Times* is going to do."

"We already know, McLeod. You're skating where the signs say not to. I guess you know that."

"Won't Wainwright be here? Ask him."

"Don't know if he will or not." One of the younger gunmen had circled around behind McLeod. The other one stood facing him, pointing the parabeam at his chest. The older man seemed to be enjoying himself.

"I don't want Spurgess killed," McLeod said. "That's the truth. I came here to prevent it myself."

"Can you tell me why?"

"No—yes. Because I want to accept Wainwright's proposition. The *World* said I was going to die. Wainwright offered me life."

"We know that you're going to die."

McLeod sucked in his breath. This same wholesome trio had probably received the application for his own death, had probably studied his habit file. "Not before next week," McLeod said.

"Now, I don't know. It's a gift horse, guy. They won't hold up our checks for a couple of hours either way."

"No, but you'll spend the rest of your life as a gunman if you cross Wainwright."

The voice behind McLeod's back seemed bodiless and as cold as the falling snow. "What's wrong with that?"

"You wouldn't understand," McLeod said without turning. "He would." He would win his life the moment he won over the shorter man. His two companions did not matter. "Look. The Gunman Editor on the *World* is near retirement, isn't he? You look like you've been around, but you won't be considered for the job if Wainwright bears a grudge."

"He's pretty smooth," the young gunman with the parabeam said.

"Why do you think I'm here at all?" McLeod insisted. "I didn't know you were coming. I came to prevent this thing myself."

THE man behind McLeod muttered a curse and said, "You came here for the same reason you always go out on an assignment. To get the story."

But the older man said, "Have you any proof?"

"Only Wainwright. Ask him when he gets here."

"*If* he decides to come," said the man with the parabeam.

"And if he doesn't?" McLeod demanded. "Are you going to take a chance and—"

"It wouldn't be taking a chance at all," the older man told McLeod. "We could freeze you and box you and ask Wainwright about it later."

"You fool! I haven't told Wainwright one way or the other yet."

"Then we could unfreeze you and let him decide. Go ahead, George."

McLeod could never hope to freeze all three of them before they froze him. Their actions were cut from the same Kantian categorical imperative he had expected of himself and all newspapermen—until today. He felt sorry for himself because it no longer applied, but that hardly helped.

"Someone's coming," the voice behind McLeod said. He started to turn and got three quarters of the way around when the parabeam hit him.

After that, it was almost like watching a melodrama on television. He could watch the action unfold. His sympathies might be directed first one way, then another, but he had no part in the play. He was a statue, standing upright as the snow drifted down and coated him with white. His body-heat didn't escape the insulined jumper to melt it and in a few moments he was an incredibly manlike snowman with a human face. The last thing he wanted to do was stand there, frozen, and watch.

He stood and watched.

Half a dozen figures were clustered close by the white columns at the front of Mayor Spurgess' house. Then, as if they were puppets and all their strings had been pulled at once, they darted behind the columns.

The *World* gunmen were caught in the open and knew it. Para-beams hissed as they fell toward the ground and the snow's protection. Only the shorter, heavier man tried to get up, waddling three or four yards on his knees before a parabeam caught him too and froze him.

Two figures detached themselves from the white columns and ran across the snow toward McLeod, parabeams ready.

"Hey, he looks familiar."

"That's Darius McLeod, stupid. Familiar, the man says. They probably caught him and froze him."

A beam sucked the sleep from McLeod's limbs and he was soon massaging his arms together. After two freezes in as many evenings, he'd really have a parabeam hangover in the morning.

"What about those three people, Mr. McLeod?" the man who had unfroze him asked.

"A natural," the other one said. "Here's our accident. Assault and robbery and accidental death. We even have the assailants. Strip these people of their *World* identification. I'll be right back—with the mayor."

NEWSHOUNDS might trick and maim and kill one another, McLeod knew, but never frame other newspapermen for civil crime. You had to keep the public happy with all newspaper people. The police, of course, never investigated very thoroughly these days, since that would be poaching on newspaper territory. They handled traffic very well, though.

There was a commotion in front of the mayor's house, where only one of the gunmen was visible. Presently the door opened. There was loud talking, much pointing. The gunman's voice was pleading, the mayor's was indignant. Finally, the mayor ducked inside and McLeod hoped he would stay there. Soon he emerged, however, dressed in a jumper. He ran along at the heels of the gunman and neared McLeod just as the other man had finished removing identification cards from the three still figures.

"McLeod, is that you? I knew I could depend on you. You have no idea how much better I'm able to relax now. No, sir. If you said I don't have to worry, I don't have to. What's going on out here? He said you wanted to see me but couldn't move from the spot. Something I can do? What's wrong with them?"

There were not three figures in the snow, but four. "Take a look," the man with Mayor Spurgess said.

The mayor waited for McLeod to answer him, then shrugged and crouched. It was exactly as if he were still under the parabeam, McLeod realized. There was nothing he could say, nothing he could do.

The *Star-Times* gunmen had sized up the situation too well. The three men from the *World* were as good as dead now, which would make it close to impossible for McLeod to turn on the *Star-Times* and expect help from Wainwright, even if that were what he wanted. He had better play along. It was still a show on television and he could only watch. But now he knew the outcome.

The fourth still figure on the snow suddenly errupted into violent motion. A leg snaked out, an arm—the mayor grunted and fell, staring mutely at McLeod, surprised, offended and outrageously indignant the moment before he died. A knife flashed quickly, expertly, gleaming for a split second before it disappeared through the mayor's jumper.

The standing gunman twirled his parabeam to full intensity and sprayed the *World* men with what was now lethal radiation, halting involuntary actions such as blinking—and breathing.

The gunman smiled at McLeod. "Well, you have your story now. We'd better get out of here while you phone for the police.

McLeod had his story, all right. He felt sick. He would call the police and then go write his story about how Mayor Spurgess had chased three unidentified vandals from his house, only to be stabbed to death while protecting his family. McLeod who was visiting the mayor on business, had naturally joined in the chase, in time to overtake and kill the unidentified vandals but not in time to save His Honor's life.

The police investigation, if any, would fail to uncover anything.

"Thanks a lot," McLeod said.

"Don't mention it." The two gunmen ran to join their companions and soon disappeared through the snow.

In tomorrow's *Star-Times,* McLeod would be a hero.

CHAPTER SIX

"ENOUGH snow for you?" Overman asked jovially as McLeod removed his jumper the next morning in his office at the *Star-Times*. "We're ready to stop it now because the *World* weather bureau finally owned up to its red face. Thirty-two inches."

McLeod nodded. He'd had trouble reaching the slidewalk through the drifts and more trouble struggling through the few yards of high-piled snow to the *Star-Times* building.

"Rewrite showed me the story you sent in last night, Darius. Wonderful... Someone over at the *World* must be biting his fingernails. They've got to be ready for split second changes in the newspaper business, though. If they don't, they're lost."

"What's that little bit of homely philosophy leading up to?" McLeod wanted to know. Overman rarely made his point without prefacing it with some mundane generalization. The more important the point, McLeod knew from experience, the triter the generalization.

"We've done a little G-2'ing these last few weeks, Darius." Overman seemed almost on the point of prancing nervously like an anxious racehorse at the starting gate. "I couldn't tell you until it was certain. Harry Crippens is a member of the Anti-Newspaper League." Overman grinned like a yawning owl. "Close your mouth, Darius. Stop gaping. It's the truth."

"But that doesn't make sense, chief." McLeod figured it made very good sense if Overman said so, but he needed time to collect his thoughts.

"Dirty doings at the *Star-Times*," preached Overman. "It's frightening, isn't it? If you can't trust your fellow reporters, just who in the world can you trust? You see, it's not merely Crippens. There's an Anti-News cell here.

"They usually work in pairs, Darius. One to get the information, another to see that editorial policy is not carried out. Don't ask me why they do it. Mis-guided anarchistic tendencies, I suppose. The first member of the pair very often poses as a turncoat with some other newspaper."

"I don't get you."

"It's simple. That way, he can play two papers against each other and try to make them both wrong. In this case, she can. You see, Crippens' confederate is our number one co-respondent, our own Miss Tracy Kent," Overman finished melodramatically.

"Tracy! That's incredible." *Don't think*, McLeod told himself. *Don't think and let it show on your face. Just listen.*

"At this moment, the *World* believes Kent is on their payroll. Kent keeps them informed of what's going on over here and draws two salaries. Crippens is her executioner. Crippens, for example, sees to it that Congressman Horner doesn't commit suicide."

TRACY had put two and two together with a blithe ease that had left McLeod wondering. Tracy had seemed to be aware of the alternative that Weaver Wainwright had offered him at the Fourth Estate. But Tracy hadn't balked because she was a loyal member of the *Star-Times* staff. She should have favored the plan, anyway, since it meant saving Crippens' life. But she hadn't favored it at all.

Because she'd held out hope for McLeod?

"How did you find all that out?" McLeod demanded.

"We suspected someone. We didn't know who. We planted television receivers and let them talk. Darius, I think you know my position. I'm a newspaperman because I think the public is so muddle-headed and mediocre it can't make its own decisions. Democratic governments try to make those decisions and fail because the people play too large a role and mess things up. Totalitarian governments fail because they're too obvious, especially when the guy next door happens to live in a democracy.

"The answer is the obvious evolution of the newspaper to policy-making journalism. People don't associate us with policy-making any more than they think short story writers or television scriptwriters develop schools of psychology. We're both before the fact and after the fact, but they wouldn't believe that if we ran it in banner headlines.

"That's what the Anti-Newspaper League is after. They don't want us to look forward. They don't want us to predict the future and then make it happen. They make inane pronouncements about the essential dignity of man and the necessity for him to work out his own destiny. They sneer at Ortega y Gasset and deify Tom Paine. They shun the concept of authoritarianism in any form and blandly forget that Mr. Average Citizen has always yearned for his little niche in a totalitarian system because he actually wants decisions rained down on him like manna.

"I hate them, Darius. It isn't logical, but I hate them. Between you and me, I would like to strangle them with my bare hands, slowly, forgetting I am a civilized man, forgetting even that we can still use them. But the opportunity is a magnificent one. You could spend all your life G-2'ing after Anti-News people and come up with nothing but wrongos. From now on they'll be playing their little game where I can watch it."

"What about my obituary?" McLeod demanded. "It's the first of the week. I thought you said we were going to substitute Crippens for me."

"I did. I still do. Cripp we will have to sacrifice. But—I apologize in advance, Darius, because I know you won't like this—our G-2'ing was thorough. We received in your apartment, too."

"Don't tell me you can't trust me?"

"Calm down. That's just it, I can. The cell is spread thin at the *Star-Times*, so thin that we'll have to watch our step until it's uncovered. You see, Darius, you are going to take Crippens' place in it. When Cripp dies Tracy will turn to someone for sympathy. If it looks like you tried to save Cripp because you believed as he did—well, I'm sure you see the possibilities."

McLEOD nodded vaguely. Anti-News. He was playing the game, almost, the way he felt. But he lacked the name. It was strange how you could amble cheerfully through life accepting or ignoring certain things until you woke up one morning and everything looked different. Whoever had decided leopards don't change their spots was all wet.

"...sorry if this sounds cloak-and-daggerish," Overman was saying, "but don't tell anyone. I can trust you. If the conspiracy is as big as I think, the good people at the *World*, the sensible ones, can probably trust a man like Weaver Wainwright. The rest must be suspect."

McLeod grinned. "Why trust me, chief?" he said easily, "I've never been a bug for ideology either way."

"That's precisely why. Newspapering is a *job* with you, but a good one. You're our highest-paid reporter. You have a reputation to maintain. A man gets muddle-headed if he starts delving too deeply into ideologies. He's afraid to see black-and-white because the other muddle-heads insist there are such things as grays. You follow?"

"Yeah," said McLeod. He followed, all right. It was all right if you thought for yourself, according to Overman, provided you didn't think too hard. You could attend all the highbrow confabs you wanted, safe in the security of your tailor-made answers. Never doubt. Never guess. You know. You just know. This is so and this is not so and there's never any in between. The insistence on shadings of opinion between truth and error was a stumbling block in the path of knowledge. Gray was for people who didn't know the truth about black and white.

"Yes, I can trust you. Thank heavens for that."

"I ought to get a raise," said McLeod, smiling and playing the role Overman had selected for him.

"Very funny. You ought to get a move on. We still have to worry about Wainwright and his men. There's no telling when they'll strike."

"So I have to strike first, at Crippens."

"Naturally. Have you filled out an application on him?"

"No," McLeod said easily, and raised a hand for silence when Overman was about to start yelling. "It's too important. I want to do the job myself. It's my life we're playing around with."

"I don't know if I approve. There's something to be said for professional efficiency. The gunmen know their work."

"I don't care if you approve or not. It's my life."

"You see, Darius. That's what I like about you. You always know where you stand."

"Thanks. I'll need some security, though."

"Now I don't follow you."

"Some bargaining power. In case I'm not as efficent as your gunmen. The proof that Tracy Kent and Harry Crippens are Anti-Newspaper."

"It's safe."

"I've got to know more about it."

"On the contrary. Simply carry this weapon with you; if there's trouble, have them contact me. Or contact me yourself. But that would ruin everything, Darius. I suppose if you have to bargain for your life, you wouldn't care."

"That's right. I wouldn't."

Overman chuckled. "You're a good man."

"And one who knows black from white, remember? Let's be honest with each other, chief. You're lying to me. You really figure if I fail, I fail. You wouldn't be willing to bargain in my behalf with what you have, and you know it. If I can kill Crippens and give Wainwright his substitute story and win Miss Kent's confidence, you'd love it. If I can't, you'll try to find another way. Sure, you think I'm good. But you know I'm expendable."

Overman thumped him soundly on the back. "Darius, we should have been brothers. Is there anything else?"

"Yes. How long would you want me to play this Anti-News game?"

"Until we get all the facts."

"Too dangerous," said McLeod. "Unless you make it worth my while."

Overman hadn't stopped grinning. "Maybe you will get a raise, at that."

"Not maybe. Definitely. Twenty per cent."

"Twenty?"

"Twenty."

"All right, Darius. Twenty it is. You'd sell your mother, wouldn't you?"

"Don't have to worry about it. The Anti-Newspaper League hasn't that kind of money. You're safe."

"I knew it," Overman said. "I couldn't have picked a better man."

"I'll keep you informed," said McLeod, and put on his jumper. He walked out congratulating himself on the way he'd convinced Overman.

Only trouble was, he now knew there was more than black and white in the world but wasn't sure he knew what to do about it.

CHAPTER SEVEN

"I'M sorry," the recorder said when McLeod called Tracy's apartment. "Miss Kent is not at home. Is there any message?"

"No," said McLeod, then lied: "This is Harry Crippens talking."

"Miss Kent left a message for you, Mr. Crippens," said the recorder. "She will wait for you at the Fourth Estate. She says it is important."

"Thank you," said McLeod. "If Miss Kent should check in, will you tell her Darius wants to save Cripp's life if he can? Will you tell her Darius has come to his senses?"

"Darius wants to save Cripp's life if he can. Darius has come to his senses. Yes, sir."

McLeod had left the *Star-Times* after a hurried lunch in the newspaper cafeteria. He'd placed the call to Tracy's apartment from his own because the wires might or might not be tapped in his office.

Suddenly he began cursing silently.

Overman had rigged receivers in various apartments—including Darius'—to uncover the Anti-News cell. If Overman had heard his conversation with Tracy's recorder, Weaver Wainwright wouldn't be the only one gunning for McLeod.

He found the receiver rigged to his TV set, unhooked it, but the damage had been done. He doubted that Overman would constantly monitor the set, yet Overman would see the damning evidence eventually. McLeod could save Cripp's life by simply not killing him, but then what? He smiled grimly. It posed a considerable problem for Overman too, for the

City Editor wanted to dump a fat wrongo in the *World's* lap but now would also want to see McLeod dead. One seemed to preclude the other...unless Overman decided to give McLeod a week of grace, then kill him. McLeod was still smiling. Perhaps the situation confronting the fictional lady-or-tiger man had been more aggravating, but it was less deadly.

McLeod taped a second parabeam to his right arm and took the escalator to the roof and his copter.

"Hi," the weaponcheck girl greeted him as he entered the Fourth Estate. "How are you today, Mr. McLeod?"

"Never better." As she approached him, McLeod removed the first parabeam from his trick sleeve and handed it to her. "I'm ticklish today," he told her and saw that she was about to say something until she noticed the folded bill wedged between trigger and trigger guard. She nodded, patted his shoulders quickly without searching, and wagged away. It happened all the time, McLeod knew. He wouldn't be the only one.

"You hurry up inside," the weaponcheck girl called over her bare shoulder. "They're doing a combo-tease."

As McLeod made his way through the darkened room, he saw a well-built man and a delightfully built women performing the combo-tease on stage. Sweat glistened on their sleek dark skins as red lights shifted and flowed across the stage. It was more suggestive than French pictures, combining features of an Apache dance and a conventional strip. It had been outlawed everywhere but at the Fourth Estate—and it had everyone's rapt attention.

Everyone except Cripp and Tracy. McLeod found them in a distant corner of the great room, hunched toward each other across a small table and talking in low tones.

"Mind?" McLeod asked.

"You have your nerve," Tracy hissed at him, but people to left and right were muttering angrily at them as the combotease neared its conclusion. "Well, I guess you're harmless enough in here."

"Sit down," Cripp said.

"Overman knows about you two," McLeod told them quickly. "The works."

"You mean that we're going to get married?" Tracy demanded. "It's no secret."

"I mean that you belong to the Anti-Newspaper League. Tracy, you're pretending to spy on us for the *World*, he knows that, Cripp, you thwart bad news when you can. You both belong to the Anti-Newspaper League. To Overman, you're both anarchistic. He'd like to see you dead."

The woman on stage had seemed spent but now rallied and held her own as they danced a frenzied Apache battle from wing to wing. Tracy, who was facing the stage, said, "That's positively lewd. We've all degenerated so much, Cripp."

McLeod shrugged. "Overman would say that's part of your Anti-News tendencies."

"And you?"

McLeod grinned. "I'm not much for spectator sports."

"No, I mean about the Anti-Newspaper League. I'm not admitting anything, but I just wonder what you think."

"You wouldn't believe me."

"Why don't you try us, Darius?" Cripp suggested.

"You don't have to admit anything," McLeod informed them. "Overman plugged a receiver into your TV sets and monitored them. Mine too, by the way. I called you a while ago. Which put me in hot water too."

"You mean he'll monitor the call?" asked Cripp.

"Maybe he already has. You can check with your recorder if you want to, Tracy."

"Tell me what you told the recorder?"

"That I was going to try and save Cripp's life. That I had finally come to my senses, I guess."

"All you have to do to save Cripp's life is nothing. I was told by someone on Lantrel's staff that you hadn't applied for Cripp's death."

"Another part of the cell," McLeod mused. "Just how extensive is it?"

"I wouldn't know," Tracy told him coolly. "Anyway, you said Overman knows."

"He does. I don't."

THE Apache strippers had leaped from the stage and now were cavorting acrobatically about the dance floor. A single red spot followed them as they pounced after each other, working their way toward the rows of tables and then among them. McLeod heard quick, eager breathing in the shadowy audience.

"I never knew they came off the stage," Tracy said.

McLeod winked at her. "Maybe one of these days they'll want audience participation."

"Very funny. If you're telling us the truth, Darius, what are you going to do?"

"You tell me. Overman wanted me to kill Cripp, win your confidence and take Cripp's place in the cell. I had to make it look like it wasn't me who did the job. But if Overman monitored my TV, he'll realize I'm not his boy. He'll have to do without an informant. He knows I'm wise to him but probably doesn't want to know. Which means he'll have to act fast."

"But if he eliminates you, Wainwright and the *World* get their scoop," Cripp pointed out.

"I know, I can't figure it. Overman's got a man-sized problem, but so have you. I don't think you have much time to leave the city. Get lost somewhere. Change your names. Anything."

Tracy bristled. "We haven't admitted a thing."

"There's no time for that. Please, Tracy," Cripp pleaded. "I think Darius is on our side. We're making a mistake if we reject him."

"Unless I'm wrong," McLeod said, "Overman hasn't told anyone but me. He just doesn't know who to trust."

"So he settles for Mr. Judas Iscariot himself," Tracy said.

Cripp slammed his hand down on the table and drew angry oaths front the tables around them. "Cut it out," he said. "Let's listen to Darius. Can you think of anything else to do?"

"Well—"

"If I'm the only one he told," McLeod went on, "and then if he found out about me and decided to come here in a hurry, we can hope he hasn't told anyone else. Chances are, he hasn't. If he found out he can't even trust me, he won't know which way to turn, not until he clears this whole mess up."

"What are you driving at?" Tracy asked him.

"Reporter, City Editor…it's close enough. Maybe Wainwright can still get his story."

"You mean Overman? You wouldn't dare."

"It isn't just Cripp's life, or even yours, if you still have your mind made up about me. It's my life too. If we can make Wainwright settle for Overman, all this doesn't have to go any further."

"What's your price?" Tracy demanded.

"For Heaven's sake!" Cripp cried.

"I can't blame her, Cripp. I was pretty nasty about it before, and I tried to be pretty tricky as well. I'm still all mixed up. I think I know where I stand now but I can't guarantee anything."

"You mean after all this is over you're liable to change your mind again?" Tracy asked him, giving Cripp an I-told-you-so smile.

"No. Definitely not. At worst, I'll be neutral. At best—"

"At best," Cripp finished for him enthusiastically, "you'll probably be made City Editor in Overman's place. You're the obvious man for the job, and if you could see your way clear to joining us, there's no telling what we might accomplish. Don't you see it, Tracy?"

"All I can see is the combo-tease. They'll be dancing on our table if they come any closer."

THE team struggled three tables away to a subtle, wild, barely audible rhythm. The man had regained the offensive, but it had cost him everything he wore except for a pair of tight trousers and one billowing, ruffled sleeve, which flapped ridiculously from shoulder to wrist.

At the last moment, McLeod thought he saw a leather strap under the sleeve. The couple had reached their table; the man forced the woman back over it, still dancing. The red spotlight winked out like a snuffed candle flame.

Tracy screamed.

The audience had interpreted the darkness and Tracy's scream as the act's final, breath-taking garnish and now buzzed in isolated knots of whispered excitement before the applause rolled deafeningly across the room.

McLeod leaped to his feet, groping blindly in the darkness with his hands. He heard Cripp shout Tracy's name and began to yell himself for someone to turn on the lights. Something struck his head above and behind the right ear and he felt himself falling to his knees. He grabbed at air, then made contact with two bare legs. Still yelling, he guessed it was the woman—then felt unseen hands tugging at his hair, fingers raking his face. He got up and was grappling with a supple-swift invisible opponent when the lights went on and blinded him.

There were shouts and restraining arms and when he could see again the woman dancer, now almost naked, was pointing an accusing finger at him. "He deliberately attacked me!" she wailed.

McLeod wiped blood from his face and said, "That's crazy." These were more than combo-strippers, he knew. They might be in Wainwright's pay or Overman's. Either way, he was in for it. "They're a couple of gunmen," he said.

The male dancer was covering Tracy and Cripp with his parabeam, which had been hidden under the flapping right sleeve. "See?" McLeod said to the circle of people around them. "He's armed."

The crowd parted to admit the weaponcheck girl to its center. With a quick, deft movement she found McLeod's second parabeam, withdrew it and told him, "So are you."

More figures joined them, in police uniforms, the polished leather harness for twin parabeams creaking on each pair of hips, the gaudy blue and gold uniforms starched stiffly. "You're under arrest," one of them told McLeod. "You'll have to come with us."

"You're no more police than I am. Since when do police do anything more than direct traffic?"

"You'll have to come with us, sir."

"And then get killed trying to escape? Keep your hands off me."

At that moment, Weaver Wainwright made his way inside the wide circle of onlookers, his long sad nose drooping over his upper lip as he smiled at McLeod. "When our police reporter said it was you, I rushed right over."

"Sure," McLeod said bitterly. "Police reporter. Why don't you admit these people are a bunch of your killers? You've really tailormade your accident this time, Wainwright. I guess I'll be killed trying to escape."

Wainwright regarded him with bland curiosity, "What I want to know is why you attacked the girl."

"He didn't attack her," Tracy said. "I was right here."

"In pitch darkness," the weapon-check girl reminded her. Apparently McLeod's bribe had been topped.

McLEOD let his eyes scan the crowd, seeking a friendly face. Here were the minor luminaries of the fourth estate gazing upon their fallen idol. For McLeod, like Weaver Wainwright, had been almost a legendary figure. But Wainwright had engineered the fall and now, like those South American fish that can strip the flesh from a man in seconds, they clustered about McLeod's social corpse. They sensed his demise as surely as if it had been something physical. They waited with avid eyes at the bottom of the ladder for him to fall. Then each figure would ascend one wrung upward and so, each with his own capable hands and thinkwriter, control human history a little more.

If only he could somehow contact Overman, McLeod thought. How much time did he have? He wasn't sure but thought it could be measured in minutes.

"I'd like to call my City Editor," McLeod said.

Wainwright chuckled. "A good reporter to the last. But I see Crippens and Miss Kent here."

"It's my right."

"The *Star-Times* will get its story. Won't you see to that, Mr. Crippens?"

McLeod stared mutely at Cripp, who finally said, "How do you know *I* didn't attack the woman?"

The stripper pouted and pointed a manicured finger at McLeod. "It was that man."

"You see?" Wainwright demanded.

"No," Cripp told him. "It was dark. She couldn't tell. If McLeod is arrested, they'll have to take me, too."

A muscle twitched in Wainwright's face, tugging the long nose down and to the left. "Very well. But Miss Kent still represents the *Star-Times*."

Cripp shook his head. "A corespondent?"

"She's capable."

"Too damned capable," McLeod said. "I have positive proof that Tracy Kent is employed as a spy by the *World*." He turned on Wainwright with what he hoped would pass for righteous indignation. "Is that the kind of fair break you try to give the opposition?"

The encircling crowd stirred, trembling with whispers. McLeod pressed his advantage by jabbing a finger at the captain of police. "I demand the right to call my newspaper."

"Well, I don't know." The man looked to Wainwright for help.

"Never mind him," McLeod said. "You tell me. I'm within my rights as a newspaperman, or wouldn't you know about that?"

Someone brought out a portable phone and thrust it at McLeod. The captain of police looked at Wainwright, who shook his head quickly from side to side. It was all right. Sure it was all right. McLeod could make no accusations in public, the law said. If he started, he would forfeit his right to complete the call. He could tell Overman that Tracy and Cripp had him, instead, but he doubted if the City Editor would act on that basis.

Wainwright grinned. "There's your phone, McLeod. We're waiting for you to call."

"Thanks a lot," McLeod told him, and hurled the instrument at his face.

He heard a thud and a startled oath and didn't wait to see the results. He whirled and struck out with the edge of his hand, slicing it expertly at the police captain's Adam's apple. McLeod vaulted over the gagging man as he went down and plunged, head tucked against his chest and knees kicking high, into the first rank of the crowd. He fought elbows, fists, shoulders, legs, warm human breaths, reaching the front of the room and sprinting past the weapon-check arsenal and out into the green, summery glade that surrounded the anachronism of stone and glass that was the Fourth Estate.

CHAPTER EIGHT

PROTECTED by a force field, the grounds around the Estate knew nothing but summer. But elsewhere, McLeod thought as he plunged on toward the copter field, man's control over the elements vied for headlines.

McLeod saw the figure of a man up ahead as he rounded the final turn in the path, still sprinting. The man stood squarely in front of him, blocking his way with a drawn parabeam.

"Did he come this way?" McLeod cried. "Talk, man! Did McLeod come this way?"

"No, sir. He, wait a minute…" But McLeod was upon him, using the same judo-cut that had floored the captain of police. McLeod wrenched the parabeam from the man's fingers as he fell, then found his copter and was airborne by the time the vanguard of his pursuers appeared as tiny dots on the field below.

Less than an hour later, McLeod landed on the roof of the *Star-Times* building, where a slowly circling plow was scooping up the snow, digesting it and spitting out great jets of steam. McLeod doubled the speed of the escalator with his own flying feet and was soon striding across the City Room, nodding briefly to the sychophantic waves and smiles that greeted him as the *Star-Times'* ace reporter.

"Chief," he said, entering Overman's glass-walled office without bothering to knock, "the wolves are after your fair-haired boy—but good!"

"Wainwright?" Overman guessed, drumming nervous fingers on his desk.

"Wainwright. Something about attacking the female member of a combo tease. If his police ever had a chance to take me, I'd have been killed trying to get away."

"So, what happened?"

"What happened, the man says. They're probably on their way here right now. In order for me to get away, Cripp had to claim he attacked the girl too."

"That's wonderful. Doesn't that take care of Mr. Crippens for us? Well, doesn't it? Incidentally, that was a stroke of genius on your part, telling Tracy Kent you had a change of heart *before* anything happened. Paving the way, eh?"

"Something like that," McLeod mumbled. Then Overman had monitored his call to Tracy's apartment, but had misinterpreted what he heard—

"Sit down, Darius. There. Are you armed?"

"Yes, but you don't think they'd try to take me right here, do you? That would be an open declaration of war." McLeod took out the parabeam and placed it on the edge of Overman's desk.

"It would be war—unless I surrendered you to them." Overman scooped up the parabeam and thumbled it to high intensity. "At first I thought that was a stroke of genius on your part, but I wasn't sure. So I had you followed. Your conversation with Crippens and Tracy Kent was ingenius, all right. But it puts us on opposite sides now, doesn't it?"

McLeod had never seen Overman so calm. His fingers no longer drummed their incessant rhythm on the desk, his legs were still. He sat motionless, like a tri-di picture of himself. McLeod said, "Not at all. I only wanted to gain their confidence."

"The one thing that bothers me is this: it looks like I'm going to give Weaver Wainwright his story after all, although there's a chance I can save something for the *Star-Times*. I suspect he'll take you off somewhere and have you killed, but the moment he leaves this office with you, you'll be denounced in the *Star-Times*. Wainwright won't be killing a top reporter. He'll be killing a member of the Anti-Newspaper League."

"You're crazy," McLeod said. "It might have sounded bad, but it was all part of the same thing. I wanted to gain their confidence and—"

"And offer me in your place to Wainwright's hatchetmen? That's interesting."

"I was lying to them."

"No. You're lying to me. I'll tell you this, Darius. It comes as a great disappointment. Suddenly, all at once, a man finds his organization is riddled with subversives. That's bad enough, but at least he has one man he can trust. He thinks. He thinks, Darius. But he's wrong there, too. Now he can trust no one. Perhaps he'll have to fire his entire staff and start from the beginning again. But it's the one man, the Judas, who hurts most. Even if Wainwright gets you and gets his story—and I get mine—I'll never be able to trust anyone again. Don't you see the position you've put me in? I'm a lonely man, Darius."

McLEOD stood up and leaned across the desk. "We've both been playing God all our lives. What do you think happens when a God loses his worshippers?"

"I haven't lost them. Just the acolytes. There are others."

"There are the people," McLeod said. "Waiting for the medical cures we promise them but never give. The farmers, praying to their own God while we ruin their crops capriciously to scoop the *World*. The dead citizens of a dozen bombed out cities in a dozen unnecessary wars. The people who haven't read Ortega y Gasset and maybe never even heard of him and can't be convinced they're too stupid to seek their own destinies."

"Ortega was right. Mass man can't discriminate. He's incapable of logical, creative thought. He blunders from catastrophe to catastrophe and grovels at the feet of demagogues."

"He can't be herded and led to slaughter."

"He can't be the master of his own fate, you fool!"

"Perhaps not. But there are people who can create, who can lead. People who pave the way and let the masses follow where they lead."

"What do you think we do? We pave the way. We make the future."

"There's a difference."

"I can't see it."

"You don't want to. The truly creative man merely does his work. The masses will follow of their own free will. Maybe they'll follow the wrong leader as often as not, but we've still come a long way in a few thousand years. It's wrong if they're led, or pushed, or tricked or—"

"Sit down, Darius. Don't move. The trouble with you anti-news people is you're too romantic. You think because God or Nature created man at the top of the evolutionary ladder, man is good, man can do nothing but move forward in the long run. You think it's a mistake for one man—or a group of men, or an institution—to channel that movement.

"But of all the institutions in man's civilization, the newspaper is the most logical one for the job. We inform, Darius. We are the essence of life. Life perceives and, after perceiving transmits information. Or builds machines to do the job. Sensation, perception, information—the same thing. We're at the top. We belong here."

"Perception should be objective, un-colored. But there's no sense talking to you."

"Perception is never objective, my dear Darius. An individual perceives. Some men are tone-deaf, others color-blind. We all taste the same foods, liking some and disliking others. I say the newspaper belongs on the top like this. I say our creation of news is no different from the hundred varied opinions of a hundred members of the rabble. Unless it's better. We're a cohesive force, Darius. We simplify. We unite."

"You hamper and destroy."

"We don't rule by force. Have they ever tried to overthrow us? Have they? You see, they don't dislike us. They have faith in us. They can grow roots and feel secure. They don't have a myriad of possibilities confronting them. They have only two on any given subject, except in purely local situations that we don't consider important. Either the *Star-Times* is right, or the *World* is."

"Why are you telling me all this?"

"It's very important to me. I believed in you, Darius. I still think you've made a mistake. While it's too late now—you see, we can't really control *all* events, can we?—I would like to hear you admit your mistake. I can never trust anyone again."

"If I admit it?"

"I'll thank you..."

"And hand me over to Weaver Wainwright?"

"And hand you over to Weaver Wainwright."

THERE was a disturbance outside, the sound of running feet in the City Room, of many voices. Overman cocked his head to one side, listening to the tiny receiver in his ear then picking up his microphone hose and saying, "In a moment. That's right, I said let them in. But give me five minutes." He dropped the hose. "They're here for you, Darius."

"I gathered."

"Would you make a man who once was your friend happy before you go? Just tell me you were wrong. Tell me if you

73

had your way over again you would remain loyal to me even if you were confronted with the same faulty philosophical notions."

"At the point of a parabeam? What good would it do?"

"Forget the parabeam. I'm two people now. I'm guarding you and I'll kill you if you come any closer to me, but I'm also pleading with you. I'm asking you to give me my salvation."

"I wonder which one is stronger," McLeod said, standing again and leaning across the desk. "Why does it mean so much to you, chief? Let me tell you. Is it because you have doubts yourself and want me to resolve them for you?"

"Keep back, I'm warning you. That isn't it at all. You've made me lose my faith in people."

"I thought you didn't have any."

"In a few people. Please, Darius. Don't come any closer. A man has to trust someone."

"You can't do anything about your doubts. You're hoping I can."

"I'm going to kill you if you come any closer." Overman was still standing like a statue, the parabeam an extention of his right hand. It was as if he would never move again unless McLeod freed him with a word. It was as if the heart too had stopped its beating and only the lips were alive, the pleading lips, begging for a reprieve.

McLeod leaped across the desk, his middle slamming down on the hard surface, his diaphram squeezing all the air from his lungs. His fingers closed on Overman's wrist and forced it back as the parabeam hissed from his cheek.

Now the lips were still. Now the muscles which had remained so inert for many moments were writhing with activity, each individual cell adding its strength to the whole, to the wiry arms, the thin legs, the twisting, heaving torso. The only sound was the harsh rasping of Overman's breath as they grappled, tumbling over and over, rolling across the floor.

The parabeam was between them, separating their chests. Overman butted with his head, bit, gouged, used his knees and elbows while he held the weapon. The lungs filled with air—McLeod could feel the torso lifting, the ribcage expanding. The mouth opened to scream for help...

McLeod got a hand over it, felt teeth clamp on his fingers, very white, very sharp. The mouth opened again as McLeod rolled suddenly clear to avoid an upthrusting knee.

Knee hit elbow and hand tightened convulsively. The parabeam hissed against Overman's chest and up, bathing his chin and face and the lips, which instead of screaming, formed the words "tell me" and then closed slowly. Afterwards, McLeod always thought Overman's ears must have retained their sentience longest as the man died, waiting for an answer that would never come.

The door opened. People stood around, looking down at them. Wainwright. The phony police. Tracy and Cripp. Some *Star-Times* security agents.

McLeod stood up slowly, his own muscles twitching. He looked at Wainwright, then pointed to Overman's body on the floor and said, "There's your story. You were modest in your prediction. Not a reporter, but the City Editor. Dead. And listen to me, Wainwright. It's the only story you'll ever get. Try anything else and there'll be open war between our papers. You understand?"

Wainwright considered, head down, arms folded in front of him, long nose hiding lips from that angle. "They'll probably make you City Editor," he mused. "I'll take the story. You're in the clear, McLeod."

"I want to be exonerated from that false charge."

But Wainwright shook his head. "Do it yourself. You have a newspaper, too. Incidentally, how did Overman die?"

"Just say he was looking for something, something important—so important that when he couldn't find it he killed himself."

"That's no story."

"It's a story," said McLeod, "We can make it a story."

"THERE are hundreds of us," Tracy said later. "All over the country. All over the world. We're badly organized. We need organization. You're in a position to give it to us."

"Not overtly," Cripp warned. "But under cover at the beginning, until we build up strength. We'll have to re-indoctrinate young reporters and then forget about indoctrination when we can. We'll be fighting a war all our lives."

"Men like Overman and Wainwright are the alternatives," McLeod said. "I think even Overman knew, at the end, that he was wrong. But it went against everything he ever thought or believed. I almost could have been another Overman."

"You're not," Tracy said. "You just had to be goosed."

"It's going to be interesting," McLeod told them. "We'll still predict. To stay in business, we'll have to predict, at least to start with. But we'll give our scientists and social workers a free hand, and our predictions will all be practical. Do you realize there hasn't been a substantial scientific discovery put to use in the last fifty years?"

Cripp seemed worried. "Their approach is much more sensational. They'll draw the readers. But we have to—to stay in business."

"That was your trouble all along," McLeod said. "You were a bunch of snipers. I think you're wrong. What's not sensational about a trip to the moon or a cure for cancer or controlled weather that actually helps the farmers or campaigning for the better man in an election because he truly has something to offer? We're liable to put the *World* right out of business."

"We can try," said Tracy, smiling.

"Not you, young lady. No more co-respondents. How would you like to be a bonafide social worker?" But Tracy squeezed Cripp's hand and said, "No, thank you. I'd rather be a housewife."

McLeod thought he'd have to settle for loving both of them like a brother—then realized he'd be too busy to do anything of the sort.

THE END

If you've enjoyed this book, you will not want to miss these terrific titles…

WHAT WAS THERE BEFORE TIME STARTED?

When did time begin? It's easy to think that time has always been here and will forever be ticking away. But what if there was an actual origin date for the planet Earth that was far removed from the approximate date (billions of years ago) to which science subscribes? What if Earth's start date was actually within the last hundred years or so, and that everything in our history prior to that point in time never really happened; that ancient history is nothing more than a mirage, a collage of historical phantoms? Sounds incredible doesn't it? But if it were actually true, what strange force or forces might lay behind it? The answers to these questions were carefully outlined in a theory that a New York professor dumped into the Sunday feature section of a large New York newspaper one sunny afternoon. Only the good professor presented his findings not as theory, but as fact. It was a story that turned the world upside down. And soon the professor and his companions set out to prove to all mankind that they were right.

CAST OF CHARACTERS

JOHN SHARP
Johnny was a great reporter, but he'd latched on to a story that had a chilling effect on his career—and the rest of the world, too!

PROFESSOR JAMES CROCKET
This brilliant scientist and historian had come up with a cockeyed theory that literally shook the world to its foundation.

LARRY KEEN
As the editor on a big newspaper he was well-respected—and when he beckoned you with his little finger you came running.

ANN SHELTON
This twenty-five year old was very cool and pretty in her gray suits, with a remarkable brain to go along with her appearance.

BARNEY SLOCUM
As a hired gun he had perfected the "tough guy" attitude, but underneath it all was a lamb in wolf's clothing.

PINKY ROBIN
Just a little guy who'd been hired to drive a man to a lake house. What he hadn't expected, though, was to deliver a corpse!

JEFFERY PINCHOTT
He was known as a Wall Street wolf, but he never expected to be thrown to the wolves himself!

ZERO A.D.

By
ROBERT WADE

ARMCHAIR FICTION
PO Box 4369, Medford, Oregon 97504

*For more information about Armchair Books and products, visit our
website at…*

www.armchairfiction.com

Or email us at…

armchairfiction@yahoo.com

CHAPTER ONE
An Astonishing Theory

"Facts compel me to conclude that my brain was never formed for much thinking" —Charles Darwin

THE newsroom was warm, smoky, and filled with the smell of ink. The presses down in the press room pounded and rumbled as though they were trying to tear the *Daily Express* building down stone by stone. Not that it would have been hard. The *Express* is more than an institution in this town. It's been here since the first mayor was tossed out of office for allowing wide open gambling. The *Express* tossed him. It's been housed in the same grim-faced brown stone building since the first police chief lost his job for letting Mugs Malone have a free hand in the narcotic trade. The *Express* got rid of him.

You get the point. The *Express* has power and plenty of it. The *Express* takes a stand and fights to the last ditch. I, being a righteous sort myself, stick with the boss because he's that kind of a guy.

Tonight the late edition has been put to bed and only Larry Keen and myself are still holding on. I hate to leave the place at night. There's as much ink in my veins as there is blood and I hate to miss a minute because some gangster always gets his when I'm tucked into bed and I don't hear about it until the next morning.

Keen looked up suddenly from his dilapidated desk half way across the room.

"Johnny," he said, and motioned with his little finger.

Larry Keen isn't the movie version of a managing editor. He doesn't drink much and he doesn't wear a green eyeshade.

When did time begin? Where did our world come from? To find out would you have to start from scratch — Zero A.D.?

He works because he likes to work. Keen has iron gray hair, penetrating black eyes, and a hatred for wasted motion. When he beckons with a little finger it carries weight.

ZERO
A.D.

By
ROBERT
WADE

I crushed my cigarette stub out on the side of my desk, lowered my feet to the floor, and moved toward him. Keen held the telephone in his hand, palm cupped over the receiver. He wasn't smiling.

ZERO A.D.

"Talk with this fellow, will you, Johnny?" he asked. "Professor Crocket of Pinecrest University. He's no dummy, so take it easy."

That was all. I didn't have an idea in the world what Crocket wanted, but that's the way Larry Keen depended on me. If the Governor had called, he'd have said the same thing. I took the phone.

"Professor Crocket?" I asked.

The voice from the other end said, "Yes! *James* Crocket. I understand you've been assigned to interview me?"

I raised an eyebrow at Keen, but he was busy again, comparing twin-leads for tomorrow's editions.

"I guess so," I said as politely as possible. "If you've got a story we'd like to have it."

Give crack-pot or genius the same treatment is the *Express* policy. Sometimes a pretty thin line divides them.

"Good!" I liked the sincere enthusiasm in Crocket's voice. "I have what I consider a sensational story. I'm releasing it to the *Daily Express* because I admire your paper. Would it be possible for you to see me the first thing tomorrow morning?"

"Just a moment," I said, and covered the receiver. Keen sensed that I wanted his advice. He looked up.

"Crocket wants to see me tomorrow morning. Has some stuff for us. Sunday Supplement I imagine."

Keen grinned.

"I do not dictate the actions of my star reporter," he said. "How does it sound?"

"It doesn't," I said, yet I had a feeling that I ought to see Crocket. "I could run out at ten in the morning. Probably get away from him in half an hour."

Keen nodded.

"Good," he said.

I confirmed the hour over the phone, said goodnight to Crocket and hung up. Larry stared at me, a smile on his lips.

"I don't suppose this will rock the world or the *Daily Express*," he said.

I'll admit I was puzzled.

"My vacation," he explained. "It's going to start tonight, remember?"

I sat down on the edge of his desk.

"That's right," I said. Editor breaks down and goes to lake for fishing trip. "Everything lined up while you're gone?"

KEEN nodded. In spite of his fifty years and gray hair, he looked at that moment like a schoolboy. I knew the strain he was throwing off when he left for the fishing trip.

"Sunday issue is all set to ride," he said. "I'll be in Monday afternoon. You can judge for yourself the value of Crocket's material. If it's good, tell Read to sidetrack the *Fish and Fowl* article in the Supplement and put in yours."

I felt a little doubtful. I was uneasy about changing anything when Larry was away. I've been depending on him too long. Damned if I'd ruin his trip with my worries.

He ignored me then, returning to the work on his desk.

I wanted to walk out and leave him alone, but I couldn't do it. The longer I sat the more I wondered about that interview with Crocket. The man was something of a genius and I knew it. He had exploded so many scientific theories in his time that half the country was with him and the other half would like to cut his throat. Keen knew it. I think it gave him a secret kick to put me on my own like that. Finally he tossed his work aside and stood up.

"Tomorrow at this time I'll be sitting by a campfire eating fresh bass," he said. He rubbed his stomach.

"Look, Larry," I interrupted. "I don't feel just right about going ahead on my own with…"

"'Nuts!" He smiled broadly. "I knew something was troubling you. When I look at you, Johnny, I see an intelligent young giant of twenty-seven who graduated from college and should have some real brains under his brown wig. I see a pair of eyes that could analyze news as well as I can. Didn't I train you myself? You can use your own judgment this time."

I shrugged.

"Guess I'm somewhat of a baby when it comes to filling other people's boots," I admitted. "Okay, Larry, take it easy up there at the lake. Bring home some of your catch if you can manage it."

We shook and he promised to pack some bass on ice when he came in Monday. The presses were turning over at full speed now. The office quivered under the force of the vibration. We went down the narrow, ink-blackened stairs to the street. Outside, the trucks were just rolling in for the morning edition. It was noisy at the front of the building, but a block away night made everything still and deserted.

I left Larry at the corner and caught a cab. Then the reaction set in. There had been a reason for my nervousness about the Crocket article. I wanted to tell Keen, and sometimes, after all hell broke loose, I think he might have suspected all the time.

The nervousness had been caused, by Crocket's parting remark over the phone.

"Be prepared," he said in a calm voice, "for an article that will rock the thinking world. An article that will shake even the honest, solid, foundations of the *Express* to the core of its editorial heart."

A speech like that from a man of Crocket's mental caliber should have been a danger signal I could spot a mile away.

Twenty-four hours later, it *couldn't be stopped.* Yet, I'm not sure to this day whether or not I'm sorry I went against my better judgment and printed James Crocket's world-shaking article.

CHAPTER TWO
Dynamite Explodes

"If I am wrong, the sooner I am knocked in the head and annihilated, the better" —*Charles Darwin*

A GLIMPSE of *Who's Who* told me that Professor James Crocket was approaching his fifty-fifth birthday and had been credited with a long and successful career. He taught a variety of subjects at Pinecrest University, which was recognized as one of the top rank colleges of the Middle West. Having gathered what little information I could from the reference library, I called Ann Shelton, set our luncheon engagement ahead to one o'clock, and hailed a cab.

Fifteen minutes later we were winding up through the wooded hills of Pinecrest Township toward the college campus.

Pinecrest is one of those evergreen hidden retreats that would make any man feel a little better for just being near its old ivy covered buildings. I paid off the cab and watched it slip down the drive and out of sight among the trees. I stood for some time, hesitating, before going in. That nagging, uneasy feeling came back. I knew before I pushed open the glass door of the Administration Building that I should turn around and run to beat hell back to my own little world of petty crime and human failure. As I went in, I removed my hat, and my hand on the brim was cold and wet.

I learned at the information desk that Crocket had a free hour between ten and eleven and had left word for me to come to his rooms. A student guided me across the campus and into a small, redbrick building well hidden behind the new, more carefully planned structures. Not that Crocket's quarters were neglected, or in any sense, had the atmosphere of alchemy and mystery. Instead, the building I found myself in was small, two-storied, and held a dignity that comes after being lived in constantly for many years.

We walked along a short hall, to a sunny, pleasant laboratory at the rear of the structure. The student knocked on the door then scuttled away as though his life depended on getting out of sight before Crocket appeared.

The door opened and I found myself facing a tall, smooth featured man. His eyes were gray and his hair, the same color, looked as though it had been carefully washed and combed just before I came in. He extended a frail, very white hand.

"John Sharp?" he asked.

"That's right, sir," I said. "I tried to make it by ten o'clock on the nose."

He looked at his wristwatch and smiled.

"Perfect timing," he said. "Come in. I'll try to take as little of your time as is possible."

That was welcome news. It branded him as a gentleman. Most of the feature stuff we picked up had to be gathered after long arguments and cut to pieces before publication.

The laboratory wasn't much. It contained a few benches, dozens of test tubes and several machines arranged along the inside wall. They made no sense to me—at the time.

We found a couple of tall, uncomfortable benches near a table. I put my hat over a test tube rack and we sat down. For some time Crocket continued to stare at me. It gave me time to size him up as a human being. I knew he was wondering just how to approach me. His hands, though strong and firm, made little fluttering motions on the rough tabletop. At last he looked at me full in the face and treated me with one of the most friendly smiles I've ever seen.

"I think," he said, "that I'll tell you the whole story and let you use your own judgment."

Somehow it sounded very flattering, as though he saw something in me that prompted his trust.

"Thanks," I said. "Knowing nothing of what you plan to tell, I can't promise that I'll merit your faith in me."

HE ROSE and went to a steel filing cabinet. He came back and dropped a sheaf of papers on the table before me.

"When I've finished, I want you to take this file with you. Read it carefully and don't pass judgment on what I have to say before you've had a night to sleep on it."

This, I thought, is rapidly growing into something big. Bigger, perhaps, than I can handle.

"To begin with," Crocket went on, "forget everything you ever knew or think you knew about yourself and the world you live in."

That was a pretty big order. I waited.

"The world is an experiment," he said. "A cold blooded, scientific experiment."

"I can understand that." I smiled. "There's nothing very settled about this world or life on it."

Crocket's expression changed. He ignored my remark. His eyes flashed with sudden fire. He leaned forward, his hands on the table, head bent forward toward me.

"Wait," he said, and his voice sank to a whisper. "Don't comment lightly on what I'm about to say. You, like the others, do not understand. I think that if you listen closely, you may be able to digest more than the average person."

Another left-handed compliment to my appearance. I was secretly pleased.

"We have always been taught that the world, *our* world, is a sort of superior sphere, blessed with many things all for the comfort of man, the almighty creature."

I had to admit that the human animal usually saw things in a light of their benefit to himself. Crocket was talking swiftly now.

"We have tried for centuries to unravel the mystery of our past. We have sought secret meanings from remote turns of the jungles. We have excavated lost cities, argued over them and rebuilt them. Each time, we try to explain our presence here as being a great improvement upon the past. We are perfect, we think, having built up gradually from weaker people of weaker worlds."

"Wait," I protested. "I'll admit that it's been pretty much of a shot in the dark, but surely scientists are getting *somewhere?*"

"Hear me through," he begged. "We have our pyramids, our snake god, our Atlantis, and the countless other bits of a huge puzzle that we try year after year to fit together. We search for missing links, and new wonders. For keystones to turn in the lock of time and bring back a complete story of the past. Why? To explain to ourselves where we came from and satisfy our minds that we are justified in having the terrific power that we have been blessed with."

I could understand what he was getting at. I had often thought that if man would look more to the future and less to the past, we would not be encumbered so much by ancient history and could go forward to bigger victories in the future.

"I'll admit that ancient history is somewhat of a puzzle," I said.

Crocket nodded. It was an automatic movement, as though his mind heard me and his ears didn't.

"A puzzle that will never be complete," he said.

He startled me. What was on this man's mind? I had to get to the bottom of this at once. I didn't have to ask. He exploded his bombshell.

"Actually there is no puzzle," he said. "It is man-made and created in our own warped, environment-controlled minds."

He had managed to stir me deeply. Something told me that he was both sane and very clever. He believed what he said, but just what was he trying to say?

"The world is an experiment," he went on. "Otherwise, how do you explain that in every case of exploration, with books or actual ruins, we come, sooner or later, to a blank wall? Men have dreamed of Atlantis and never turned the key in its door. They have found clues to ruins of so many and varied types of civilization that they cannot probe deeply into any of them. If the unexplained secrets of the world were put into books, it would take centuries to unravel and isolate a few facts. Then we would only be on the outskirts of the real problem."

"And if we did unravel them," I asked with sudden spirit, "where would we be?"

He shook his head quickly and I saw that he was pleased.

"Exactly," he said. "Why not look to the future? Environment holds us down with chains of the past. We mutter darkly about lost races—hidden civilizations as powerful as our own. We worry about the missing links.

"If we solved every problem, what would we have? A few more libraries of ancient history. Yet, if we could turn to the future, forget our environment, and practice with that same untiring effort to improve ourselves, some real good might eventually come out of our race."

I'M NOT a scientist. My imagination is limited by meeting a certain quota of headlines every day. Yet, his argument sounded convincing.

"Just what is *your* explanation?" I asked.

"Simply stated, it is this," he said. He used his words carefully, spacing them, not so much to gain effect, but to keep his own mind clear. "The Earth was placed here at a very recent date. It was set in motion with a number of people upon it."

"Inconceivable," I said. "Remember that you can't explain away what is in rock. That you can't burn the books that have lived for us. That we have ancestors to remember."

"You manufacture synthetic materials in a laboratory, don't you?" His voice was as cold as ice.

I nodded.

"Then consider a vast civilization, advanced millions of years beyond our own. Imagine the workmen of this civilization making in their huge laboratories a synthetic world. Perhaps this globe is small. We have nothing for a comparison. Now, just as a relief map is made, these men of science built up a world, layer upon layer. They put on it all the things we have grubbed for and brought to light. They have placed in our minds the belief that we could remember things that we cannot actually remember. They gave us a complete history.

"Actually, none of these things are true. We think we remember our childhood, our ancestors. We believe we are being clever to dig up bits of our puzzle and analyze them.

"But here is the perfect explanation. The *only* thing that will explain why we are constantly faced with bits of the puzzle of life that cannot be assembled.

"There is no puzzle at all."

I shook my head.

"Sorry," I said. "You are sincere. I believe that, or I wouldn't listen to you. Yet, you can't explain away the facts we are sure of. The idea doesn't ring true."

He wasn't angry. He looked discouraged, but unbeaten.

"What do you know about the pyramids?" he asked.

"Why," I hesitated, "they were built as burial places for the Pharaohs back in—I think it was 3200 B.C. They…"

He nodded.

"I know the common conception of their origin," he said, "yet, as with other discoveries, has man even been able to explain them to his full satisfaction? Has man ever been able to explain any of the world's wonders in a way that *everyone* could understand?"

I shook my head.

"And if man succeeded in doing so, would it make any difference to the worker who struggles for his daily bread? Would it conceivably improve his future?"

I grinned.

"It would make damned fine headlines," I said.

That brought the first smile I'd seen in half an hour.

"Headlines," he repeated softly. "Think what startling headlines I could make if I could only prove…"

He shook his head.

"I cannot expect you to believe everything I have told you," he said, "but, you came for a story. Print it in the Sunday Supplement, with your articles about wives who have five husbands and babies who are controlled by ghostly hands. Print it and let them laugh at it. I'll have one consolation. I've *tried* to get my idea across, and though I have failed before I start, I'll know that I'm right."

I FOUND my pencil and a notebook. I turned an eighth of an inch of lead out of my Eversharp and waited.

"The world has no past." He talked smoothly now, as though reciting a lesson he knew well. "Perhaps ten or even twenty years ago the world was tossed into space from a planet far advanced in its thinking. It hung there in void and started to spin. It was a model, made of substances that can be combined in any laboratory. On it were the false remains of puzzles that no man will ever solve. Man and woman were placed on its surface, and into their minds, false memories were placed.

"These men and women were given memories. Memories that told them *they* were all powerful. Memories that made them think they had a past. They were given books, homes, and material things. Their bogus memories told them that *they* had been responsible for history.

"All this was done to find out if man would fit into his environment and struggle with the unsolved puzzle, or if they would rise above this and see that a huge hoax had been perpetrated against them. Would they fight to free themselves of the bonds that had been placed upon them?"

"But why," I interrupted desperately. "If it were possible, what would it all net the power that put us here? What is the end of the plan?"

He sighed.

"If I knew," he said, "I for one would escape before it is too late. I would take those with me who have the intellect and foresight to understand me."

He shrugged.

"For those without the blessing of imagination, I could do nothing."

He stopped talking. The room was deathly still. The sun came in, sending shafts of light across the desk over my cramped writing fingers. The light startled me and brought me back to the present. I stared around at the clean, barren room.

"Then according to your theory," I said, "none of this was built or conceived by you and me. It was prepared for us and we were tossed into it like animals into a cage, to see if we could find a way out."

He nodded.

I stood up, shook hands with him, and put on my hat.

"I'll print it," I said. "It will make a sensational story. I can't promise that it won't hold you up to criticism."

He smiled. I knew that he was smiling at me and not with me. He held the same respect for me as he did the remainder of the people on planet Earth.

"Take the papers," he said. "Today is Friday. You don't have to write your story until tomorrow. Make me one promise. Read this entire file and then use your own judgment. I won't expect more than fair treatment."

I took the papers and put them into my brief case. He escorted me to the door. Once out in the sun, the full power of my imagination started to play hell with me. There's something about the enormous strength of the subconscious mind. Where the ordinary, everyday thoughts leave off, the subconscious, mind takes over. It won't listen to reason, that is, not everyday reasoning. It fights its way ahead, ignoring the narrowness of the body it is contained in.

By the time I hailed another cab and was on my way back to town, I was a mental wreck. I knew Crocket's story *couldn't* be true. A lot of people have expressed odd theories. You can't believe them, but just try to toss them aside, and bingo, they hit you like a ton of lead.

BY the time I reached the *Express* Building, my hands were actually a little sweaty. I felt nervous. I half expected to see some huge, all-enveloping eye staring down at me from the sky. I went in, fought off the temptation to tear

Professor Crocket's papers from the brief case and start reading them; and finally decided to call Ann.

She was waiting for me at her office. Ann is a dress designer, and a damn good one. She's a real pal too, but Ann wouldn't be in a mood to listen to what I had to say right now.

Her voice was warm and eager when I reached her.

"You've been a very poor luncheon date, darling," she scolded. "You're an hour late now."

Startled, I glanced at my watch. More time had been consumed with Crocket than I had ever dreamed. I apologized and we talked for a while about pleasant things. A home, a garden, all of which Crocket wouldn't have been much interested in. Then, when I should have rushed to her office and taken her out for an extra large steak, I did a strange thing.

"I'm sorry about lunch, Ann," I said.

"It's never too late," she reminded me. "I'm still hungry and unfed."

I felt miserable, but my briefcase was open on the desk and Crocket's file stuck halfway out of it.

"Larry Keen left last night," I said, "and his desk is piled up with details. I'll have to forget the pleasure of eating with the world's sweetest woman, and work right through until tonight."

Her words didn't betray the disappointment that was evident in her voice.

"Then tonight, perhaps?" It was almost a challenge. "Dinner at the Wentworth and a show afterward? If you're broke...?"

I felt like a heel.

"Tonight, at eight," I promised. "And I'm *not* broke. If you don't cut out—!"

She laughed and everything was all right again.

"I guess being a business woman isn't good for me," she said. "I'm so independent with money that I forget my sweetheart still has pride."

We hung up soon after that and I plunged into the file of Professor Crocket's papers.

It was twelve long hours later when I put the last well-thumbed sheet down again. Twelve hours filled with emotions that I had never thought to face. The *Express* was alive and humming as usual. However, to me the building had lost its life. It was a dead, sterile monument, placed here by something and given a background and history by a power greater than the world. *Greater than the ant who calls himself man.*

Emotionally, I was a wreck. Professor Crocket had won a follower and Larry Keen had lost a damned good reporter. From now on my stuff would have a different color. The color of a synthetic, test tube world, in which man continually fights to establish himself and solve an impossible riddle.

CHAPTER THREE
After Effects

"I am very poorly today, and very stupid, and hate everybody and everything. One lives only to make blunders" —*Charles Darwin.*

I MUST have been in a trance, as I remember little of leaving the *Express* Building and arriving at my room with the portable typewriter in one hand and James Crocket's file of papers in the other. I do recall Mrs. White, my landlady, bringing up a pot of coffee, as she always did when my typewriter clicked into the wee hours. Then the phone rang and I was suddenly pulled from my work by the scruff of my neck, remembering that Ann and I had a dinner and show date. I looked at my watch. It was midnight. I hated to answer the phone, but knew it would only make matters worse. Ann knew my habits well. She should have. We planned to get married in the spring.

I picked up the phone and said, "Hello."

"For Heaven's sake, *Mr.* Sharp." It was Ann all right. Her voice wasn't very pleasant. "Are you going to make a habit of standing me up?"

I stammered a poor explanation, and I'm sure Ann must have got the impression that the papers I was working on had priority over everything else in the world. When I finished, I still had said very little. Perhaps I could explain later. To try now would be a hopeless task.

"It didn't matter very much anyhow." The way she said it, I knew it mattered very much. "As it turned out, I didn't suffer."

A pang of something akin to jealousy shot through me. I'm afraid I let my voice grow a little cool.

"Just what do you mean by that?"

She laughed and it had an unpleasant, almost triumphant quality.

"Have you ever seen the lobby of the Wentworth after eight in the evening?"

The question wasn't necessary. We had both eaten there often.

"I have," I said bluntly.

"Well, it's loaded with sailors and soldiers. Some of them are officers, and very intelligent men."

I should have kept my mouth shut. Suddenly I saw red.

"And I suppose you looked very lonely and sweet?"

Ann was enjoying herself, or pretending to. I wasn't sure which.

"After all I had been stood up twice in the same day," she said, and there was a pout in her voice. "His name is Jerald Connover, and he's a lieutenant. It was quite harmless, the dinner and the dancing."

"Quite," I said angrily, and hung up. I was bitter and so damned mad I couldn't think straight.

Suddenly I hated everything, everyone. I hated the world and the smug little people on it. I hated Lieutenant Jerry Connover for taking my girl out to a dance.

It was in that mood, distrusting the world and the people in it that I sat down to write Professor James Crocket's expose of a bogus, *ersatz*-world. The phone tried to interrupt me three times after that, but I ignored it, taking a certain delight in returning some of the bitter tea Ann had made me drink. In my mind, although I could offer her no explanation, I was justified in forgetting her. Never had anything shocked me so much, and I knew that never again would I be so deeply moved as I was that night.

I didn't stop writing until nine o'clock Saturday morning. The room was cluttered with balls of tightly wadded paper that I had torn from the portable and tossed around me. Cigarette stubs littered the dresser, the rug, and even the bed. My coat and hat were on the floor where I dropped them as I came in.

Mrs. White came in at nine, after knocking timidly. She gasped with horror as she saw the mess.

"Mr. Sharp," she was instantly worried over my health. "Coffee, all over your shirt. Are you ill?"

I stood up unsteadily while she rushed to the window and threw it open. I motioned toward the untidy stack of stuff that I had written.

"Sick to death," I confessed. "Sick of men and the world in general.

I TURNED away from her and went into the bathroom. I knew I had to take a shower and awaken myself enough to make the trip to the office. When I came out, I felt as I imagine a man might who has been run over by a steamroller and straightened out again by a blacksmith's hammer. At least I had put on a fresh shirt and taken a shower.

Mrs. White was gone, but the neatness of her was reflected by the missing cigarette butts, the loss of the empty coffee pot, and the sun that streamed into the room, desperately fighting the acrid fumes of dead cigarette smoke.

I managed to stay on my feet long enough to deliver my story to Reed and tell him to run it in place of the *Fish and Fowl* article. Reed is a smart little guy who recognizes sensational stuff when he sees it. He read two paragraphs and looked interested.

"Lot of screwball junk that our fourteen year old readers will swallow in a gulp, huh?"

I nodded, too exhausted to explain.

"Run it in two installments," I said. "It'll sell extra copies next Sunday if you plug it."

Somehow I managed to find my way back to the boarding house. The room smelled fresh, and Mrs. White had been up again to straighten up the bed. It wasn't necessary. I remember taking off my hat, sitting down on the edge of the bed to fumble with my shoelaces. That was all.

When I awakened, sunshine was streaming through the curtains. My suit coat was arranged neatly over the back of a chair. My shoes were under the bed, and I knew that the mothering spirit of Mrs. White had been on duty once more. I turned over carefully, experimenting with each muscle and decided finally that I would be able to move once more. I had that terrible coffee and cigarette taste that develops when a man's stomach is allowed to repose on the same level with his head for several hours.

Up to now, I hadn't thought of anything important except that I was awake and wasn't sure I liked it. Then my eyes lighted on the neat stack of Crocket's papers on top of the dresser. My typewriter was there also, and half a pack of cigarette.

Professor Crocket's Papers.

Damn it. Forever after that I was to connect a very special group of emotions to living every time I saw or thought of Crocket. Right now, I wasn't sure of myself. I felt as though I had taken a huge bite of some strange new food, was unable to spit it out, and as yet wasn't sure that I wanted to eat it.

That, perhaps, was as close as I would ever come to understanding the strange man and his work.

I found the bathroom unoccupied and spent twenty minutes soaking under the shower. After that I felt much better. I shaved carefully, knowing that it must be Sunday, and returned to my room. The clock in the hall pointed to two-thirty.

I dressed, hesitated over calling Ann, and decided against it. I was still strangely angry about what had happened, although I wasn't sure which of us had the best excuse for being upset.

Quite often on Sunday afternoon, I wander into the *Express* office and spend an hour or two gabbing with the boys. It acts as sort of a club meeting because none of us have a great deal of time to talk about anything during the remainder of the week.

I went downstairs, into the sunlight of Bracey Street, and wandered slowly toward the park at the end of the block. A yellow cab swung out of the park and I hailed it. The driver pushed the door open. He didn't look very happy. I assumed that someone had made him drive them all over town and he was angry at having to go so far from the center of town. Drivers are like that most of the time. They make more money on a number of short trips.

I got in and leaned back, trying to review at long distance the emotions that had poured through me while I wrote the

"Papers of Professor Crocket." The theory still hit me like a ton of bricks. It was impossible to take a calm, third person look at my thoughts.

The driver caught my eye in the rear view mirror. Finally he spoke, "You read the papers today?"

I shook my head.

"Been sleeping overtime," I said. "What are the Russians doing to the supermen?"

He shook his head. "Plenty," he said, but that wasn't what he had on his mind. "Say," he went on, after a minute's hesitation, "what you think about this world. It's anchored pretty tight, ain't it?"

I DIDN'T understand. I said so. He actually blushed.

"I mean, well, there ain't no danger of us sorta getting all tangled up in our environment, whatever that is, and falling and breaking our damned heads, is there?"

I was beginning to see the light. I was understanding, through my first contact with the world since Saturday, that my article had caused some excitement.

"If you mean the end of the world, I don't think you have to worry," I said. "I guess we're safe enough."

I saw a smile come over his face. His chin relaxed and he grinned.

"Some damned screwball on the *Express,*" he said, "is saying that we're done, all washed up. 'Lay down, brother,' this guy says, 'you're dead.'"

I tried to keep my voice as calm as possible. I hadn't dreamed that my article would produce *this* effect.

"What—what sort of a story is it?" I asked. "Who wrote it?"

The cab driver shook his head.

"Some half-baked ninny named John Sharp," he said, and there was a hint of anger in his voice. "The *Express* calls it 'The Papers of Professor Crocket.'"

"Oh," I said, and shut up. My face was red. It *felt* red, though I couldn't actually see it. I don't know at that moment whether I was ashamed or just plain frightened. I knew that if a cabby; driving around the park had been so strangely stirred, what the effect would be on the middle class, to whom most copies of the *Express* were peddled.

"Anyhow," the driver added, "I don't know much about law and stuff. If this guy Crocket can be sued, they oughta take him for everything he's got. A guy ain't got no business scaring people like that. It—it ain't moral."

He had spoken his piece and he felt better. We were in front of the *Express* building now. I jumped out, paid my fare, and almost ran toward the door. I was so excited that I forgot to tip him.

CHAPTER FOUR
I Lose a Good Job

THE newsroom was humming with activity. For that place to buzz on Sunday was a miracle. The Monday editions went to bed late. We all stalled for as long as we could, evading until the last minute, the business of starting a new week.

But this was different. *How different I realized the moment I poked my head in the floor.*

Larry Keen was back. He sat with his head resting cupped on his hands, his telephone removed from its cradle.

I heard the undercurrent of voices as I went in. Larry sensed the change and looked up. He saw me and his face was gray, dispirited. He looked as though he'd been dragged through a heavy fog and absorbed it into his complexion. His eyes met mine and wavered.

"Johnny..."

That was all he said, but it was enough. I've known Larry a long time. He had never acted like this before. I went over to his desk and sat on the edge of it. I took one of his cigarettes from the tin of flat-fifties.

"What brought you back?" I asked.

The questions wasn't necessary. I think I knew.

"You guess," he suggested.

The room was deathly silent now. A couple of the new boys hung around. The older men drifted out, in respect to me.

"The article?"

He nodded and didn't say anything at once.

After a while, he said, "Johnny, why did you do it?"

I was beginning to resent what was happening. I hadn't rested long enough yet and a lot of things were still mixed up in my brain. One thing I was sure of, in spite of how I hated to hurt Larry, I knew in my heart that I was right. Larry had meant for me to treat the Crocket article with my tongue in my cheek. I had written what I *had* to write, a sincere explanation of Crocket's research, and a firm argument in his defense.

"Look here, Larry," I said, "you told me to use my own judgment. I did."

To my surprise, he didn't blow up. He continued to stare at me and his eyes were red.

"You probably *thought* you were sincere," he said. "Now look at my side of it. I was enjoying myself up at Lake Weller. The fish were biting and the paper was all set to take care of itself. This morning, I get a wire from Johnson..."

"Johnson?" I interrupted. "He didn't...?" Oland Johnson owned the biggest share of the *Express.*

Larry nodded. "He's up in that air to stay," he said. "Gave me hell for letting you go ahead when I was away."

"I'm sorry, Larry," I said. "I shouldn't have done it, not until you got back."

He grinned, but it wasn't a very happy expression.

"Forget that part of it," he said. "Johnny, why did you do it? Why did you get taken in by some crack-pot professor?"

"But he isn't," I protested. "Crocket's right. He has firmly convinced me. After checking on his research, there can be no doubt."

He made an impatient motion with his hand.

"Forget it," he said. "I read the article. With your name on it, it's dynamite. Look here, Johnny, you've been under my wing for ten years. You've developed into the best man I have, and because of it, I give you a lot of privileges. This time…"

"I've stepped out of bounds," I said.

He nodded.

"You understand, don't you, that it's not me who has the final word? You've attracted the attention of the big boss, and I'm only his stooge."

I nodded. I felt too low to talk. No use pretending that the *Express* wasn't a part of me. Being fired was no fun.

I reached for Larry Keen's hand and we shook.

"No hard feelings?" he asked.

"None."

He stood up.

"Hell," he said. "Let's go out and get drunk."

WE SAT alone in Brett's Bar, a popular little place that leans against the right side of the *Express* Building. It was four o'clock. For the past two hours I had been trying to convince Larry that Crocket was right. I insisted that my article was based on facts as reliable as any scientist had been able to present.

We were both mellowed by several scotch and sodas. I was making headway, in spite of Keen's hard headed, everyday news views.

"But you can't say that he's absolutely right any more than you can say that the others are wrong, There's no way of proving definitely that Crocket is on the right road. If I can depend on what you've said, the world won't end or anything of that sort."

I thought I understood Crocket's mind pretty well, considering the short time I had known the Professor.

"No," I admitted. "But, it's the environment business again. We'll go on fighting, not forward, but backward. When we should be planning for tomorrow and building up new plans, we continue trying to reconstruct our past. We are tied to the past. Take war for example..."

I was warming to the subject. It was like a spark that grew and grew inside me until my whole mind was on fire.

"We fight a war. Someone who thinks more clearly than most of us says: 'Why are we fighting? What's the object?' The answer is...there have always been wars and we have always fought, from the beginning of time. That we can't escape war. And that's only one point. Hundreds of men with brilliant minds spend their entire lives digging into the past. Why not forget that past? A past we never had. Why not devote more time to perfecting the thing we have and forgetting the ape and the fish we were supposed to have been at some murky uncertain time in the past?"

"Then Crocket's theory is that we are living under a curse?" Larry added. "A curse that was passed to us by some race of super-men on another planet? That we haven't any past? That our books, our memories, even everyday things are bogus? That they were manufactured and placed here to confuse us?"

I nodded.

"Confuse all but those who have the sense to realize that this tangled, patchwork past means nothing. That it can never lead us anywhere but to further misery and uncertainty. Our minds are all tied up in dusty books and dustier memories. They are entombed in the very ruins that we dig from the earth."

Larry chuckled. The Scotch was good. It made my head lighter and the room, warm and friendly. Brett, the proprietor of the bar, set up drinks on the house. He leaned back once more to listen to us. His small, red eye-had never left my face since Larry and I started to talk.

Larry tossed off his drink and stood up.

"It's unfortunate that you can't talk to each subscriber of the *Express*," he said, "You might convince them."

He then hesitated, staring at me.

"Just as you've convinced me," he added.

Brett cleared his throat and leaned over the bar. "And me too," he said in a strangely moved voice. "If I tried to preach that stuff over the bar, my customers would throw me out. But, Mr. Sharp, if you need a few bucks to get by on, let me know. Tell that Crocket guy that I'm on his side. I'm gonna forget all about the past and start looking ahead."

"Suppose you could forget the bill?" Larry suggested.

Brett grinned. "That ain't far enough in the past for me to forget," he said. "But the drinks are on me—today. If you don't get another job pretty soon, Mr. Sharp, come around. There's always pretzels and sandwiches here."

I assured him solemnly that I would, and we left.

Larry hesitated on the sidewalk.

"Where are you going now," he asked? It felt nice to have him worrying about me.

"I've got to take Crocket's stuff back to him," I said.

"Stop at the office tomorrow," Larry said. "I'm going to talk with Johnson again."

"Don't do it," I begged. "It's only hurting you. Johnson's sore at me. There's no sense to your getting on the wrong side of him."

"I'm going to talk to him," he said. "S'long."

"S'long," I said, and wandered up the street. I turned around when I reached the corner and stared at the rough, dirty front of the *Daily Express* Building. The trucks were beginning to move out with the morning edition. The sun was low and it hurt my eyes. I rubbed them with the back of my hand and plunged blindly away toward home.

CHAPTER FIVE
Ann Explains

GOOD Lord, how it grew. The momentum of it was slow at first, like a well-formed sphere of snow starting down a long hill. At first the kernel of the idea was clear. Then, gradually, as people of all types applied their own meaning to the story, the thing became wild and uncertain. The sphere rolled faster and faster, gathering in size and growing hazy with the many interpretations applied to it.

I felt it, late in the afternoon, downtown. The *Movie-News* had recognized the story's value and tossed together a film on the subject. It was advertised all the way across the side of the *Movie-News* Building.

"EXPRESS PRINTS DARING STORY"

Come In and See the Film That
Will End Your Doubts

I read that the film was accompanied by Hanz Kalterburn's voice and that the charge for the show was twenty-five cents.

I paid my quarter and heard Kalterburn's voice before my eyes adjusted themselves to the darkened theatre.

"The idea is utterly fantastic. Men in high places have for centuries explored and re-explored our wonderful world. Every ruin tells a story. Every book gives us a picture of the past or the present. To arouse such doubts in the minds of our people in time of war is sabotage."

For a miserable half hour I watched bits of old exploration films the Movie-News people had been able to assemble. The pyramids, the lost cities of the Aztecs, the Pueblos of the Southwest. Kalterburn's voice pursued me through it all.

"You see with your eyes" material things that this man says do not exist."

Crocket had said no such things. He had not denied that the ruins were there; that the books were in print. He had simply denied that they meant what they seemed to mean.

"The reporter who covered this story and the paper that allowed it to go to press should be ousted from the Association. Such men are winning the war for the enemy."

The film ended. Some of the people who saw it shouted and stomped their feet. The lights came on. Others sat very still, their faces deathly calm, as though they were trying to think for themselves. I stood up and left. Behind me, the blare of military music filled the theatre. Another film, the story of MacArthur came on to the screen.

I wasn't trying to sabotage the war effort. I wanted America to win, with every bone in my body. I had written dozens of powerful stories about the war. I had been congratulated on doing a good job. Now this one article had hit me below the belt. The city, perhaps the world, was against me.

I couldn't escape.

The moving lights on the *Evening Mirror* Building flashed above the Square. The lights spelled out news-leads to advertise the *Mirror*. The *Mirror* hated Oland Johnson and the *Express*.

I watched as the sign flashed out its message. Others watched also. People jostled me, but I stood there looking up.

"NEWS ISN'T NEWS WITH *EXPRESS*—PAPER PRINTS WILD STORY—FABRICATED FROM STAR DUST AND IMAGINATION—PLAYS ON IMAGINATION WITH SENSATIONAL LIE"

I doubled my fists and moved into the early theatre crowds along the street. Everyone was talking. Papers were a sell-out. Everyone expected more comment. They got it. I bought a copy of the *Mirror*.

Every columnist in that tabloid was out for the blue-blooded *Express*. The front page was covered by a huge picture of the pyramids. The headline was simple and a masterpiece.

ARE THE PYRAMIDS AN OPTICAL ILLUSION?

I crumpled the paper and dropped it on the sidewalk. I went home.

PERHAPS I should have called Ann Shelton. Usually I could have found comfort in her voice because she could straighten me out faster than anyone I knew. It wasn't any use. Yesterday I had acted like a fool and I knew it. I envied Lieutenant Jerry Conover. Dinner at the Wentworth and dancing afterward. I wondered bitterly if the Lieutenant could dance. I'm a flop at it. Perhaps they had made another date for tonight.

I flopped down on the bed. The phone rang, but I couldn't find the courage to answer it. Mrs. White usually came up in the evening and talked over any stories that carried my by-line. She was white-headed and a sweet old lady. She seemed almost like a mother to me. Tonight she didn't come. Probably thought I was out I tried to tell myself. Still, my light was on and she could see it from her room.

The phone rang again at nine o'clock, but I was undressed then, staring up at the ceiling and trying to go to sleep.

Then I was dreaming about a huge ape that flung himself down at me from the top of a vine-covered tree of the past. The ape stood on the bed grinning at me.

"I'm your great, great, great, great, great grandfather and then some," he said. "Remember me?"

"Go away," I pleaded. "You don't exist."

He got a hold on my arm and twisted it back until perspiration stood out on my face.

"Try to explain that away," he said. *"You can't get rid of me. You can't throw away the past."*

It was as though I was coming out from under ether. Bells were ringing and they slowly turned into voices.

"The past— You can't throw away the past—past— past—past—"

Then I was awake. My arm ached because I was laying on it. I heard the voice again, Mrs. White's voice.

"Past dinner time, Mr. Sharp. I saved something for you. You didn't come down."

I felt all choked up inside, but I was glad that she had awakened me.

"I—I'm not feeling very well," I said. "Went to bed early. Thanks for thinking of me."

"You're sure you won't eat some toast if I bring it up?"

She sounded very sad.

"No thanks," I managed.

I heard her footsteps die in the hall. It was very quiet outside. It's always like that on Sunday night. People are tired out, gathering strength to fight the new week. I didn't have any fight left in me.

Larry Keen was on the phone. "Dammit, Johnny," he sounded angry. "Just because you're on the spot you haven't any right to ignore Ann. She's been a peach. Why don't you call her? She's going crazy."

I tried to sound cold and disinterested. "I don't think she's interested in what I'm doing," I said.

He fairly exploded.

"Don't be a ten-year-old," he snapped. "Ann told me that story of the Lieutenant. She thought you'd take it as a joke. There isn't any Lieutenant. She felt badly when you didn't show up. She invented the 'other man' to tease you and you swallowed it like a puppy swallows marbles. Get wise to yourself, will you?"

Before I could answer, he added, "She tried to call you several times and you weren't in. She got frightened and contacted me."

Larry, Ann, and I were together most of the time. He was like an older brother to her. She went to him when she thought I needed more help than she could give me.

"I guess I've made a fool of myself," I admitted. "I was tired out and the Lieutenant story sounded like the real thing."

"Forget it," he advised. "Call Ann. I'm still working on Johnson, but I'm not getting very, far."

"Larry—you shouldn't."

I stopped. He had hung up.

I HAD been awakened by the phone.

It was Monday, the first working day of the week, and I had no job. I started to dress, but I felt so darned good about the non-existent Lieutenant that I couldn't wait to call Ann. I picked up the phone.

"Parkway 3224," I said.

In a minute Ann's warm eager voice greeted me.

"Johnny?"

"I was wondering what you were doing for lunch," I said. "Just in case you feel like taking another chance with a heel."

Her voice broke and I knew she was trying to keep from crying.

"Johnny," she said. "You poor darned fool, you, you...I'm waiting for you. You didn't think...?"

"I thought I was God Almighty himself for a couple of days," I said, "but a few other people have ideas too and they have knocked me off my self-made throne."

"I want to talk about that," she said. "But first, please come down right away. I can eat a second breakfast. Besides, it's after nine. I'm getting hungry."

"So am I..." I said, "...to see you again. I'm on my way."

That was the shortest shower I ever took. I was dressed and in a cab before the clock passed the fifteen-minute mark. Ann is no dunce. You might get the idea that because she likes to have me around that her I.Q. wasn't so high, that I was just one of her weaker moments. Otherwise, Ann was twenty-five, very cool and pretty in her gray suits and she had a remarkable brain.

She had used that brain. In five years she had built a business around her ability to design clothing and sold her designs to the best tailors in the country. Paris will come to Ann for dresses eventually and be glad to get them.

Her office was small and tastefully decorated. Ann was standing behind her desk, her fingertips on the glass top, waiting for me as I came in. I felt like a kid who comes home after running, away to seek new adventures.

"Gosh," I said. "You, look good." I never think very clearly when I'm with her.

She came around the desk and I acted more like an octopus than a man. Her hair smelled sweet when she pressed her face against mine. Her lips were made up in perfect cupid bows, but I put an end to that. She struggled weakly for air, and when I saw she was smothering, I let her escape to arms length.

"That was for the lieutenant," I said. "May he never do so well."

Ann blushed.

"I didn't really…"

"I know," I said hurriedly. "Larry called me. I've been a jealous dope."

She smiled.

"Maybe. I like you that way," she said. "At least you cared enough to be angry."

"It wasn't that." I remembered Crocket and the trouble he'd sent my way. "It was the story I was working on."

Her eyes clouded. She returned to the desk and sat down. I followed her and sat on the wide windowsill looking down on the busy street.

"I read the story," she said, and her voice was low. "Johnny, didn't we have an understanding?"

I nodded. She meant this business of me rushing off, half crocked, and making a fool of myself. This wasn't the first time. I was always writing something that turned out to be dynamite. I had lost several chances for promotion.

"I guess I really took care of the wedding date this time," I said. I had a lump in my throat that I couldn't swallow. I felt foolish.

DID you have to do it?" she asked, then before I could speak, she smiled again and it was like the sun coming out. "I guess you did," she confessed. "Poor Johnny. You have to champion some sort of cause or you aren't happy."

She reached up and stroked my forehead. I know how good a dog feels when you pet him. Her fingers were cool and soft on my face.

"I know I'm a damn fool," I said, "but Crocket's a swell person. The least I could do was write something that wouldn't make people laugh at him."

"But that article." She shivered. "You don't actually believe what you said."

I felt my chin growing stiff. With anyone but Ann, I'd have had a fight on my hands in two minutes.

"I believe every word of it," I said. "And there's another installment that is more startling—believe me—than the first."

"It won't be printed, will it?" she asked.

"Not in the *Express*," I said. "Johnson and his customers have taken care of that."

She shook her head rather doubtfully.

"The things you said give me the creeps," she admitted. "You can hardly expect me to feel good about the thing that lost you a job."

We were waiting for one more raise. I had refused to accept her money and now it looked as though another year or two lay between us and the cottage on the hill.

"I'll get something right away," I promised. "There are always better jobs if you look around hard enough for them."

"Not with Larry for a boss, and the *Express* to hold you up. You hated to leave, didn't you?"

There was no point in hiding the truth from her. "Next to losing you," I admitted, "it was the hardest thing I ever did. They gave me a couple of shots in the arm once, and they used printer's ink instead of blood. It's better than blood for me."

It wasn't any good going on like this and we both knew it.

"Let's eat." She tried to act bright and happy once more, but I could see the worry-lines on her forehead. "I had a single egg for breakfast and its strength is wearing off."

I kissed some more of her lipstick off and she applied fresh make-up. We went downstairs and ate in the grillroom.

CHAPTER SIX
A New and Bigger Job

I HAD the odd feeling that I was returning to the scene of a crime. Pinecrest University looked just as calm and pine hidden as it had when I visited it the first time. That's where I was wrong. Pinecrest could stand the charge of dynamite that Crocket had set off. The college had been there for half a century and it took more than Crocket to move it from the map.

Pinecrest didn't ignore James Crocket, however. It removed him to save its own reputation. That, I am told, is known as "saving face."

I found my way to the weather beaten building that housed Crocket's laboratory. I knocked and he came to the door. To my surprise, he looked quite happy and contented with the world. You'd never have guessed that he had just returned from a long and unhappy grilling before the Board of Directors.

"Come in, Mr. Sharp." He shook my hand hard with enthusiasm. "It seems that you decided in my favor. I'm afraid we've exploded something powerful under the noses of some important people."

I agreed that we had, and found myself in the sun-lighted lab once more. I waited for him to lock up the papers I had returned.

I was going to tell him about the greeting I had received at the *Express*. I didn't have to. He went to the window and stared out for a long time. He came back and his face was sober.

"It's going to be hard to leave Pinecrest," he said. "I lived and loved it here for many years."

"They evidently gave you the same treatment I received," I said.

He nodded.

"I'm accused of preparing sensational drivel that will undermine the reputation of these fine halls of learning," he said. "It didn't come as much of a shock. I spoke, not entirely willingly, to Oland Johnson of your paper. He insisted on immediate action and sat in on the hearing himself. Mr. Johnson informed me that you have also, as he termed it, been 'given the gate.' "

"For keeps," I said. "We are now two men without a country."

His eyes grew stern and uncompromising.

"Not entirely," he said. "Fortunately, the press, although not entirely free, has done a fine job for us. We have come a long distance toward awakening the imaginations of the people." I was puzzled by his reference to "we," as though he considered us partners.

"I'm glad, somehow," I said, "that I did a good job. That is, I guess the job must have been good to get such speedy results."

He smiled openly. "You are my first convert," he said. "I'm thankful that I gave my papers to a man who understands, them. I took that chance."

"And now we can both go on relief and spend our time digging, even though it probably won't be for ruins," I said.

Crocket chuckled.

"I think not," he said. "That is; not if you'll listen to my proposition." This was the second time he had linked us together. Frankly, I was curious. I had fought for him and his theory. I wanted to be in on the finish. I knew that Ann didn't approve of him. She had said as much. Yet, I admired him greatly and felt that we were destined to be close to each other. I didn't have to question him as he volunteered information.

"I have a comfortable cottage on Lake Speer, Minnesota he said. "It's an out of the way place. I planned, some day, to present my work to the world. I knew when that time came, I'd have to leave here. I made a home for myself at the lake. I'm not a rich man, but I have a few thousand dollars in the bank. I also have a complete laboratory and some highly complicated machinery at the lake."

He paused to catch his breath. He spoke now with the eagerness of a man who is anxious to see his work accomplished.

"Come with me for a few weeks. We'll prove that your article was not false. That we both know what we're talking about."

The idea sounded fine. Yet, I had to get work. Ann asked me to waste no time, and I owed that much to her.

"I planned to take my fiancée to Saratoga for two weeks," I said. "She has an uncle there and we both wanted to get away. After that, I have to find a new position."

Crocket put one hand on my shoulder.

"I hate to lose you," he said. "You're the only person thus far who has grasped what I am trying to prove. Couldn't both of you come up to my place? Perhaps, in two weeks, we can go a long way toward presenting definite proof that I'm right. There's good fishing, swimming, and boating at Lake Speer. I'm sure it would, be an ideal arrangement."

He smiled a little woefully.

"I'm sorry I can't hire you as an assistant. I haven't the financial means to pay you a salary, but I can feed you plenty of good food."

I told him I would call Ann. Secretly, I hated to part company with Crocket. He had become a symbol of truth to me. A man who dared face the world with what he believed, regardless of the greeting he received.

Ann realized the mental condition I was in. I think it was her wish that I settle this thing once and for all, in my own mind. She didn't pretend to agree with Crocket. In fact, she had made up her mind that she couldn't like the man who had influenced me so strongly. However, because Ann is naturally unselfish, she consented to changing her plans and going up to Lake Speer. Upon questioning Crocket, I found that Speer was a small, spring-fed lake in Northern Minnesota. We could fly to Twin Cities and take a train from there.

"Outside of my own cottage, the only people on the lake are at a small camp about a mile away. In the summer a group of religious fanatics come up to relax and blow off steam. But they never trouble me."

He was wrong. We were in for plenty of trouble, and not solely from the camp. Other people visited the lake that summer. People who never dreamed of going before the printing of the first installment of "Professor Crocket's Papers."

CHAPTER SEVEN
A Visitor—with a Gun

ANN and I stood on the beach watching, as the big speedboat cut white furrows across the blue surface of the lake. It turned a wide circle and came directly toward us. We had arrived at Lake Speer the night before. Professor Crocket's cottage turned out to be a brown-shingled affair, square, and with four large rooms on a single floor. There was a small lean-to kitchen against the back wall, making a fifth room, if one could call it that. With three bedrooms, and the laboratory, which we had not yet seen, the cottage was quite comfortable.

Ann suggested a morning swim, and we had been in for a short dip.

Then the motorboat roared to life somewhere across the lake and we watched it progress toward us for several minutes. It came in close, a slim, rakish craft, and rocked gently from side to side. The motor stopped and a man stood up, one hand still on the wheel. He saw us for the first time and steered the boat toward us. He was in close before he attempted to speak. When he did so, his voice was abrupt and powerful.

"You people know a Professor Crocket who's supposed to hang out up here?"

His voice was so commanding that, like a couple of children, both Ann and I tried to answer at once. Realizing how he had bluffed us, I stopped talking while Ann explained that Crocket's cottage was in sight among the trees and that we were his guests. Immediately, I was sorry that we had spoken. The boat was near us now. The stranger remained on his feet. He wore a well-tailored, cleanly pressed suit, but there his ordinary appearance vanished. He had the ugliest face I've ever seen. There wasn't a blemish on it. No outstanding feature made him ugly.

It was the power in his eyes, the coarse, dark skin, and the leering, kingly manner in which he spoke. He looked straight through Ann, as most anyone would have done, considering the small, two-piece suit of ivory color that she was wearing. He stared at me then, as a teacher would look upon a pupil in the back row.

"Thanks," he said. "Come out here and pull my boat in."

He didn't ask me. He said it quickly, and I knew if I had refused, it would have shocked him. The man had not been accustomed to receiving an argument. I don't know why I did it. I should have told him to go to hell. Instead, I waded into the water and caught the rope that was attached to the mahogany prow of the boat. I pulled it in gently until the nose touched the sand. He had stepped to the front end and as the prow caught the sand, he put one hand on my shoulder and jumped.

He didn't thank me. He didn't look back at us. He had covered half the distance to the cottage before I came back to my senses.

"Of all the…"

Ann chuckled.

"Count to ten, Johnny," she said. "That's the first time I've ever seen anyone lord it over you."

I was growing angrier by the second. I had no idea who the man was. The boat gave away nothing of his identify. It was upholstered throughout with rich, maroon leather. It smelled of money spent in huge amounts.

"If he thinks he can get away with that," I said. "I'll…"

She put a wet hand on my arm.

"Wait a minute," she said.

The man had entered the screened porch of the cottage and was waiting for Crocket to receive him. Then the door opened, a few words were exchanged and they both went inside.

"He evidently knows Mr. Crocket," Ann said. "You'd better not say anything. He may be a friend. I'd hate to have you hurt Mr. Crocket's opportunity for a new start if anything like that is afoot."

She was right. Probably someone from the University. Perhaps Crocket would have another stab at the old job.

We went in for another swim, but I felt uneasy about the whole thing. I couldn't explain why.

I either made friends or bitter enemies of any person, upon our first meeting. On a number of occasions, I've judged human nature pretty accurately. This time I knew without asking the reason why, that the man who had gone to the cottage had been bluffing. How, or why, was still a puzzle. Half way to the diving raft, I turned and struck out swiftly for shore.

"Wait on the raft," I said. "I'm going in for some sun-glasses."

I heard Ann's tinkling laughter as she reached the raft.

"Cream-puff," she called.

I REACHED the shore and walked toward the cottage slowly, so that she wouldn't be curious. Once in the shadow of the porch, I turned abruptly, slipped in among the small pines that surrounded the building, and made my way silently along the side of it. It was sandy here and my feet were silent in the sun-warmed soil.

I knew that Crocket would take his guest into the lab. It wouldn't be logical for them to talk in the bedroom or kitchen.

Although I hadn't been in the lab yet, it was located at the northwest corner of the cottage. It had two large windows that pushed outward. These were open.

I heard voices inside. Staying close to the wall, I inched forward. A thick growth of evergreens hid me from Ann's sight. I heard Crocket's voice. It was calm, but I thought I recognized an undercurrent of fear. I stood very still, listening.

"I had nothing to do with preparing this fate for the world," he was saying. "I simply analyzed it and told others what I found."

"You started the trouble," the other voice said. *"Now you'll sign this paper."*

"I'm sorry," Crocket hesitated and I heard him sigh. "I'm unable to sign." The sun was warm on my bare shoulders. I felt foolish standing there in swimming trunks. I had no weapon, nothing to protect myself.

"How about that punk out there swimming with his girl?" the stranger asked abruptly. "Is he the guy that wrote the article?"

Crocket didn't answer. There was a sound of heavy footsteps on the floor of the laboratory.

"You don't have to answer," the stranger said. His voice was as expressionless as ever. I could see that heavy set, evil face and the dark eyes that must be studying Crocket's every move. "I can get it out of the punk."

I was growing angry. I resented him and the way he spoke of me.

"I'll promise that after I've spoken to Sharp," Crocket said. "He'll refuse to deny a single word of this article. You'll find that he is intelligent and loyal enough to stand by me."

More sounds within the lab as though a chair was pushed roughly aside.

"You evidently ain't heard of me," the stranger said. "Certain business men don't think this article should be left in the public mind. It's causing a lot of trouble for these men. Contracts have been cancelled. Stocks have taken a nosedive. When the big shots get in trouble, they call on me to take care of that trouble. They put up the money for my protection and I do the rest." Crocket laughed. He refused to be bluffed.

"You can't take care of *this* trouble," he said. "A gun and a silencer might save you for the time being. You might even escape the law. You *can't* escape certain laws that were set up to control this world. One of these days, and soon, you'll pay for the fact that you refuse to believe in me."

I moved a few inches closer to the open windows. *A gun—and a silencer?*

I was glad now that I had come up to the cottage. Very glad. I looked around for a weapon. My foot contacted a large stick of firewood half buried in the sand. I inched downward and picked it up.

"You don't believe in that guff yourself," the stranger said. "Someone paid you to stir up trouble. Before I leave, *I'm taking care of you, and your friends.*"

The way he spoke, the sound of him moving around told me that I must act fast. I stepped directly into line with the open window. I saw Crocket standing with his back to a long table. The stranger stood away from him, perhaps six feet with a pistol aimed at Crocket's heart. The gun was equipped with a long, wicked looking silencer.

My shadow fell across the floor. The man with the gun whirled.

"Johnny?"

Later, I thought Ann's sudden shout must have saved my life. She had been impatient and called from the raft. Her voice was loud enough to carry inside the cottage.

"Damn…"

The man whirled and fired at me. However, Ann's call caught him off guard. He thought we were still down at the lake.

The bullet whizzed past my face. At the same time I swung the heavy stick with both hands directly at his face. He went down with a groan and Crocket took one swift leap, landing on top of him.

I was through the window and after the gun. It was on the floor near the two men. Crocket didn't have to fight. The stranger lay very still, his face bashed in, blood burbling from his mouth.

"Johnny?"

Ann's voice came again, from the path in front of the cottage.

"Nice work, Johnny," Crocket said. He went to a cabinet on the wall and found some gauze.

Swift footsteps sounded in the hall. Ann came in, fear written in her eyes.

"Good heavens—" she said, stopping short, while staring at the man on the floor. "What have you two been…?"

She saw the gun in my hands and the look on Crocket's face.

"I'm proud of you, Johnny," she said simply. "I guess I was a fool not to guess."

In five minutes we had the stranger's face well bandaged. We covered his eyes also, with a thick layer of clean gauze. I tied his wrists together with a length of rope—just in case. When he came around, I was sure that he'd think he was much more badly hurt than he really was. Warm water applied to his mouth proved that he was missing three teeth and had some deep surface cuts. With the bandage on he was blind. He couldn't tear away the bandage as long as his hands were tied.

CHAPTER EIGHT
Delivered!—One Corpse

BARNEY SLOCUM wasn't nearly as tough as he thought he was. We had him in bed with his ugly face swathed in bandages and his sting removed by taking away his gun. Barney became a quiet visitor. The worst problem we had was to find a place for him. All three rooms were full. I took him in with me and spent that night on a folding cot near the door.

Slocum finally told us his name. He had to talk, to let us know what a tough customer we had taken prisoner. He wondered just how badly he was hurt. Ann was busy with dinner. Crocket was down near the lake. He had hidden the speedboat in a heavily wooded cove a quarter of a mile down the shore and hadn't returned as yet. Barney hadn't yet divulged his name. He spoke suddenly from under the mass of bandages. His voice was muffled and he sounded less sure of himself. "Anyone around here?"

I laughed outright. This was the tough guy an hour ago.

"You have company," I said. "Would you like me to read you a children's story so you can go to sleep?"

He swore and struggled to release himself. His hands were tied to opposite sides of the bed with plenty of rope twisted around the springs.

"You wait until *they* hear about this," he said. "They'll come up here and smoke you out."

"And who are *they?*" I asked.

He swore again. I had suspected that he was a lone wolf. If, in truth, he was employed to murder Crocket, or make Crocket label his work as an outright lie, *they* wouldn't dare poke their noses in at a time like this. I've heard of big business employing killers. I've never heard of them coming to the funeral.

"Don't worry," I said. "The boat is hidden. You're pretty well taken care of yourself. No one will know you're here."

He was quite still after that.

"How badly is my face hurt?"

I told him we didn't know. There was too much blood. I said I thought his eyes were in bad shape.

He struggled to get up again, then sank back.

"Your name's Sharp, ain't it? I've seen you around the *Express* office."

He surprised me. I had never seen him before. I didn't answer.

"Mine's Barney Slocum."

That was different. I felt pretty good about bashing his face in. Although I'd never seen him, Slocum was well known for what he was. Barney had sent many a washed up political figure along the road to the cemetery. He killed, coolly and without much thought, for a price. Now I knew that no one would dare put pressure on us. Slocum was strictly a lone wolf. A dangerous one.

"Pleased to meet you, Barney," I said, "at the throwing end of a hardwood stick."

Most of the fight had been knocked out of him.

"You haven't decided to tell us why you came here? Who's paying the expenses for this ill-fated man hunt?"

He didn't answer.

I heard Ann in the kitchen rattling pots and pans. Crocket came up the path. I recognized the light footsteps on the porch. I went out to meet him.

I THINK we can make Slocum talk," Crocket said calmly. "That is, if you think it's worthwhile?"

We were just finishing up some of the finest corn bread that I've ever tasted. I decided that if Ann could make corn bread like this, I'd marry her inside of the next month. Besides, this was the first time I'd ever seen her with her cheeks red from the stove, a little red and white apron wrapped around her attractive middle, eyes snapping with adventure. The odor of pines came through the kitchen window. All in all, with Barney Slocum tied securely to the bed in the other room, it was a swell world.

An idea was buzzing around inside my skull.

"I think it would be a good idea to make Barney talk, and fast," I said. "But he isn't the talking kind. What's the plan?"

Crocket smiled. He helped himself to another slab of Ann's corn bread and broke it up in his milk.

"Part of my future depends on a machine I have perfected," he said. "I wasn't going to mention it until you two had had a day of rest. Now I think we'd better use the *Memory Finder* at once."

I remembered a long, coffin shaped cabinet in the lab. Busy with Slocum, I hadn't given it a second thought.

"The cabinet is a *Memory Finder*," Crocket said. "I spent many years developing it. I planned to use it on you first. Perhaps Slocum will make a good guinea pig."

I saw Ann's nose wrinkle. After feeding Crocket, she had fallen in love with the gray-haired, keen-minded professor. She refused, however, to have any part in his work.

"Do we have to talk about that?" she asked.

Crocket wasn't angry with her.

"I'll confess that your cooking is by far the most interesting subject tonight," he said, and his eyes were twinkling. "However, if you'll be kind to Johnny and me, I think, we can impress you shortly."

Ann reached over and mussed my hair.

"Johnny impressed me a long time ago," she said. "But I didn't do so well with him. He refuses to marry me."

I protested, and Crocket interrupted gravely.

"If I thought I was spoiling any happiness for you two," he said, "I'd send you back to the city tonight. I feel, somehow, that everything will work out for the best. Now— shall we assist Mr. Slocum in the laboratory?"

Barney Slocum lay full length inside the coffin-shaped *Memory Finder*. He had to lie still. Murder and worse was in his mind, but his wrists and ankles were firmly gripped by metal bands that in turn, were anchored to the sides of the box. Crocket wheeled a table to the side of the cabinet.

It was dark outside and wind blew in from the lake, sighing high in the pines. The lights were on and the lab was bright, almost cheery. There was nothing mysterious about Crocket's actions. He seemed to know what he was doing.

The table held the oddest-looking machine I've ever seen. It had a huge, elongated glass tube filled with red, sparkling liquid. The tube was mounted on two uprights that allowed it to pivot end over end. Underneath was an electric motor with wheels and gears attached to whirl the tube.

Crocket unrolled three coils of wire and attached them, with the aid of clamps, to both wristbands and the band on Crocket's left leg.

He turned on the power and a gauge, mounted on the edge of the cabinet, lighted. The needle quivered up and down the line of numbers. They read 1947 1946-1945 1944-1943-1942—and so on, back to 1900.

He adjusted a knob so the needle pointed to 1947.

"I think this is as far as we'll have to go tonight," he said.

Ann and I were both curious. The experiment had all the earmarks of a Mad Professor movie thriller, yet I had faith in Crocket.

WHEN the motor came on, the tube started to revolve, throwing the red liquid from one end of the tube to the other, as it turned end over end. The swish-swish of the liquid grew steadier, faster, as the motor gained speed. The liquid was a scarlet blur now. Then, to my amazement, a rainbow of color splashed into the air and hovered in a halo over the machine.

"Thought-rays," Crocket explained in a cool voice, "colored artificially by the machine, so that I can detect them."

He spoke to Slocum partly to calm him, partly for our benefit.

"The *Memory Finder* will not harm you," he said. "The machine makes you feel drowsy." The electric-ray going through your body collects thoughts from your brain and forces you to speak them aloud. When the machine stops, you will not remember what you have said. Your subconscious mind tells us what we want to know. Your conscious mind will not know that you have spoken."

"I'm not afraid," Slocum said. His voice sounded hollow and unreal.

The tube flashed around so fast that the liquid was no longer red. Colors came and vanished—green—purple—gray—yellow.

"The machine is set at 1947," Crocket said softly. "What is the important thing in 1947?"

An unmistakable chuckle came from Slocum's lips.

"You are," he said. *"You've turned things upside down. You've turned their plans upside down."*

"Crocket's voice remained calm but his face was red. His hands were shaking as he turned to me.

"This will be very simple," he said. "Then he turned and snapped a question at Slocum.

"Name the men who sent you."

Silence. We all waited. Slocum was fighting his subconscious mind.

"Name them…"

Crocket's voice was hard.

Slocum relaxed. His voice was tired, far away.

"Johnson" he said. *"Oland Johnson."*

I clenched my fists and swallowed.

"And…?"

"Johnson got plenty of pressure from the big shots," Slocum said. "He had to publish a personal apology for running the article. He has to get a signed statement from you that your papers are false."

He went on, naming names of men in industry, banking, big business.

I didn't hear much of it.

So the owner of the *Express*, Oland Johnson was responsible for this? First he fired me. Now he had tried to have Crocket murdered.

I squeezed Ann's arm and left the room. I heard Crocket switch off the machine and I knew that Ann was following me.

"Johnny—don't do anything foolish, please."

I turned and caught her in my arms. I kissed her.

"I'm on Crocket's side, all the way," I said. "Johnson tried to pull a fast one. If he had succeeded, his hands would be clean, but all three of us would be dead.

"That's all I need. The world should have a chance to read the other half of 'Professor Crocket's Papers'! People need all the information to draw a fair conclusion. Big business and lousy politicians aren't going to stop it from being published."

"But who—how? No one would dare touch it now."

I grinned. I was plenty happy.

Happy enough to kill Johnson bare handed if he got in my way. The telephone was one of those old style, crank models. It hung on the wall near the front door.

"Just watch me," I said and went to the phone.

I cranked the phone until the local operator answered.

I'm calling long distance, New York," I said. "A person-to-person call to Oland Johnson, owner of the *Daily Express.*"

I stood there waiting for them to find the big shot. I was so damned burned up and excited that my hands were shaking. I could hardly hold the receiver. Ann waited, her face very pale, her eyes on my face. Somehow, I got the idea that she was darn proud of me right now. She held up her hand so I could see it in the half-light of the hall. Her fingers were crossed.

"YES? Oland Johnson speaking." The voice was faint over the phone. I could detect impatience in his words. I had never met Johnson. He wasn't the-type to mingle with the ink slaves who ran his paper.

"This is John Sharp calling, Johnson," I said, and I wasn't careful about the anger in my voice. "I'll come straight to the point."

I heard him sputter with sudden anger. "John Sharp? You aren't the kid who was responsible for that Crocket article?"

"You're damned right I am," I said. "And I'm calling about running the second installment."

I figured that would get him and it did. When he had finished with a long choice list of oaths he said, "I told Keen to fire you."

"He did," I said, "but that doesn't prevent me from using a public phone. Now, about that second installment of 'Professor Crocket's Papers'."

"You go to hell," he said, and I knew from his voice that he would hang up in another second or two.

"Likewise," I said, "but first, listen to what I have to say. We've caught your pet, Barney Slocum. He's told everything about the deal you made him. We've put him where he can't talk with anyone. *If you see things our way.*"

I heard him gasp for his breath, as he tried to control his voice.

"I never heard of Barney Slocum," he said. "You've got some sort of scheme up your sleeve."

If he could bluff, okay. I just wanted him to know that he wasn't bluffing *me*.

"That's all right too," I said. "But if the second installment of my article isn't released tomorrow, and without editorial comment, Slocum will be in the hands of the local police. *He'll* tell a story that I can peddle to all the papers. It will put the *Express* in a deeper hole than you've ever thought of digging."

"Wait a minute," he begged. "We may have been hasty about firing you. Perhaps you could be placed on the payroll and take a vacation until this thing blows over."

"I've got ideals," I said sarcastically. "See you in the funny papers."

I hung up.

Ann grabbed me as I turned away from the phone.

"Did he promise to print it?"

I took her arm and led her back toward the lab.

"We'll know tomorrow. Meanwhile, let's see some more of that machine and what it's doing to Slocum."

The tube had stopped whirling and the power was off when we went in. Slocum was sitting up.

"Had a nice rest," he said. He was a little more friendly than he had been at first. Slocum had always dealt with men who settled their arguments with lead. He never ceased to wonder why we were so decent to him after he tried to murder us. "Guess you guys sorta flopped, if you expected me to do any talking."

Crocket turned and winked at me.

"You see what I mean?"

He had told us that Slocum would have no memories. It was true. Slocum thought he had been asleep and unable to communicate with anyone.

"It's a wonderful discovery," I said. "I imagine this was only a small example of what can be done."

Crocket nodded. Then he spoke to Slocum.

"If you'll give me your gentleman's agreement that you won't try to escape, I'll untie you and let you sit in the sun a while this, afternoon. You need it."

BEHIND the mask, Barney Slocum was silent. I could fairly hear the man's mind in action. Here were people who not only treated him decently, but offered him temporary freedom, backed by his word of honor.

"You're a funny bunch," he said. His voice was oddly strained. I knew that it put him on the spot. "Yea! I ain't ever been a Boy Scout, but if I can get a place in the sun for a while, I'll be good."

Ann rewrapped his bandages so that he could see. She helped him to a chair on the front porch. It was warm and sunny there. When I looked out a half hour later, Barney Slocum, the lone wolf and the killer was sound asleep. Killers, if Slocum was an example, snored loudly.

I returned to Crocket in the laboratory.

"We've drawn his fangs," I said. "He's resting like the 'bad little kid'."

I heard the car on the state highway almost from the time it left the end of the lake. It surprised me, because little traffic comes this way. Crocket's cottage is the only sign of habitation along the south side of Lake Speer, and our only visitor thus far had been Barney Slocum.

It must have been close to midnight.

I lay on my back, eyes wide open, staring up at the ceiling. In my bed, Barney Slocum slept soundly. We had tied him up again, as soon as night came. He was too valuable a piece of property to risk losing during the darkness.

The night was stormy. The wind howled across the lake and sent rain whipping against the windows. The door to Crocket's lab swung back and forth, squeaking a protest at the draft through the hall. Above the sound of the storm, I could still hear the car. Its motor roared loudly and I could trace its progress as it came closer.

At last I knew it must be close to the small rutted road that led to the cottage. Perhaps I wasn't too surprised when I heard the gears clash and knew it was bouncing down the eighth of a mile of rutted road to the cottage.

The sound of the car worried me. Who would be coming here as late at night as this? I arose quietly and dressed in my slippers and robe. Barney was still asleep, his arms outstretched, the knots tight on his wrists. I went into the hall. The car was close now and I watched it as it whirled into the yard, circled, and stopped with a jerk near the door; I stepped to the porch. I could hear the others moving about inside. The car had hardly halted before the front door flew open, and a rain-coated figure jumped out and dashed to the protection of the porch.

He almost knocked me over, uttered a surprised oath, and got control of himself.

"I—I gotta see Mr. Crocket," he said.

I managed to get a lantern lighted, and as he spoke, I tossed the match into the rain. I held up the light where I could see the visitor. His face was thin and covered with a day's growth of beard. I knew he was a Lake Speer product.

I had seen him working near the gas station down at the crossroad.

"I think he'll be out in a minute," I said.

I heard Crocket moving in his room.

"I'm Pinky Robin," the stranger said. "I *did* have a man who wanted to come up here. After what happened, I didn't know what else to do. I brought him anyhow."

It was a puzzling statement, and I didn't pretend to understand him. I did understand that Mr. Pinky Robin was one of the most frightened individuals I'd ever met.

"Crocket will be out right away," I said. "I don't see anyone in the car."

Robin started to shiver. He looked wildly toward the cottage, then out into the ram at the glistening car.

"You can't see him from here," he said. His teeth were chattering. *"He— It's on the floor."*

"On the floor?"

He shook his head automatically. Rain streaked down his face. *"He's dead."*

I pushed the screen door open and ran, head down, toward the car. The rain hit me like liquid ice through the thin robe. I threw open the back door to the sedan.

The figure of a man, clad in topcoat and bowler hat, slipped silently past me and hit face down in the mud.

CHAPTER NINE
Barney Slocum Escapes

I HEARD Ann's short, startled scream and sensed Crocket's presence beside me. I leaned down and turned the corpse over so that a white face lay exposed to the rain. Slowly the mud dissolved and streaked away so the features were visible. I didn't recognize him.

"It's Johnson," Crockett said. *"Oland Johnson.* He was present at the board meeting the day I was ousted from the Pinecrest staff. I'd recognize him anywhere."

Together we carried the corpse to the porch. It wasn't my first contact with death, but I had never had a corpse delivered to my door before. Ann went into the kitchen and started some coffee. She lighted the fire that was ready for morning. When I went in, Pinky Robin was sitting beside the stove drinking coffee. Crocket went to the phone. I wolfed down a cup of coffee and went to my room. I was shivering violently. The robe stuck to me and I was plastered with mud. The noise had awakened Barney Slocum. He turned his head as I came in.

"What's up?" He was friendly enough, and as curious as a schoolboy.

"Someone shot my old boss," I said.

He grinned. "Johnson?"

I said, "Yes."

He lay very still as I discarded the robe, dried myself and started to dress. Then he laughed softly.

"Ain't I glad my hands have been tied all night," he said. "And that reminds me. I'm getting tired of laying in the same place. How about letting me up for a while?"

"Crocket's calling the State Police," I said. "They'll ask a lot of questions. I'll let you up if you promise to be good. You're a guest here. Do you understand that? You don't know anything about anything."

"Good enough, Johnny," he said. "You know, I'm beginning to like you."

CAPTAIN Dave Steele of the State Police, climbed wearily from his coupe. Another trooper climbed out of the driver's seat and rounded the car. They both came in out of the rain. Steele was tall and looked much taller in the neat boots and gray whipcord trousers. He tore his trench coat off and dried his face on a towel that Ann brought from the kitchen.

"It's a hell of a night for a man to get shot." He stared moodily at the blanketed figure of Oland Johnson. We had placed the body on the porch swing.

His companion was red cheeked and a trifle chubby. He looked as though he spent most of his time behind the wheel. His uniform was shiny and worn from slipping in and out of cars.

Crocket introduced Ann and me. The Captain's driver was Jim Walters of the Highway Patrol. He said little and smiled bashfully at Ann.

"Now then," Steele said briskly, "who is this corpse and how did it happen?"

Pinky Robin came from the kitchen carrying a half-emptied cup of coffee.

"A car went by us on the road, Captain," Pinky said. "Someone shot from an open window."

Steele looked mildly surprised at Pinky Robin's presence.

"Hello, Pink," he said. "I'm glad you're in on this." He turned to Crocket. "Pink's a good boy," he said. "I'm glad you warmed him up with that coffee. I could stand some myself."

Ann went into the kitchen for some cups. Steele crossed the porch and lifted the blanket that shrouded Johnson. He took a long look then dropped it again. He whistled.

"There's something about a corpse," he said soberly, "that's so damned final." He didn't get tough like cops at home would have. He let us talk and he listened.

"This fellow came into town from the private landing field down at the corners," Pinky said. "Told me he had chartered a plane from New York and wanted me to drive him up here."

"It was raining blue-blazes before we'd come a mile. About three miles back a big car whirled by us, damned near went into the ditch, and someone shot at us from the rear seat. This—this man," he pointed at the blanket, "let out one groan and I heard him hit the floor."

Pinky Robin gulped and drank the remainder of his coffee hurriedly.

"The other car dropped behind and I—I just kept on driving."

"I think the shot might have awakened me," I told Steele. "Of course the sound must have been far away, but suddenly I was wide awake and staring up at the ceiling. Something about the car coming this way troubled me. I was on the porch when Robin drove in."

BARNEY Slocum came from the kitchen. I half-wished that he had stayed out of sight. Steele shook hands with him and he and Dave Walters exchanged friendly grins.

"I'm going to call the coroner," Steele said. "Dave, you'd better go back to town. I'll call headquarters and have all the roads blocked. You tell the boys what happened here."

Walters got into the car and vanished up the rain swept road. Steele spent ten minutes on the phone. Then he came to the kitchen. We were all staying close to the stove.

"I believe Pinky's story," he said, "so I guess that lets you people out for the time being. Any of you have a car up here?"

I shook my head. "We came in a bus from the station," I said. "Mr. Slocum hiked up from the train."

Steele nodded. "You have any idea why the man who was shot was trying to get up here, Professor?"

Crocket's face betrayed new emotion. "His name is Johnson," he said. "Oland Johnson, owner of the New York *Daily Express*. He made sure that I lost my teaching position

141

because of an article Mr. Sharp wrote for his paper. I have a copy that you are at liberty to read."

Steele smiled. "You weren't mad at him, were you?"

Crocket shrugged. "I didn't admire Johnson for what he did," he said. "But I wouldn't kill a man."

"No," Steele said thoughtfully, "I don't think you would."

He stood up.

"If you're ready to go back to town, Pink," he said, "you can drive me. I want to take a look at the car. We can do that when we get it in the garage."

The coroner arrived before Steele left. A half hour later Lake Speer was quiet once more. The rain stopped. We sat in the kitchen for some time, trying to figure out who killed Oland Johnson, and wondering what Steele had in store for us. Barney Slocum was strangely silent.

At last he arose. "Tie me up again, will you pal?" he asked me. "I need a little more beauty sleep."

I said, "Go to bed and don't bother me. I can't stand people who are always asking to be tied up."

He hesitated, then slapped me on the back.

"You won't regret that," he said and went to the room.

I was ready to turn in. Poor Ann didn't look as though she'd sleep again, however.

"Sort of a tough night, kid. Not exactly like quiet little did New York."

She shook her head. "I'm all right," she said. "It's just the coffee. It keeps me awake."

"Not to mention corpses," I said, under my breath.

"I guess I'll find a chair," I said, "lean back under a lamp, and read until morning. It might as well be in your room."

She looked grateful. "Maybe the coffee won't keep me awake, if you're around to look at," she said.

I waited in the hall for her to announce that she was warmly tucked in. The phone rang. I lifted the receiver. It was Larry Keen calling from New York.

"Hello, you old son-of-a-gun," he shouted. "Say, Johnny, what the hell did you do to Oland Johnson?"

He startled me.

"*Me?*"

"Yea," he said, and I could sense complete happiness and satisfaction in his voice. "Old Simon Legree Johnson called up this afternoon and told us to run installment two of 'Professor Crocket's Papers' on the front page of all tomorrow's editions. I was out of town and just got back. We're going to knock the hell out of a lot of people's thinking. What changed Johnson's mind?"

"I wish I knew," I said absently. "It'll be pretty hard to find out now Johnson's dead."

"*What...?*"

"He was shot tonight, sometime just before midnight."

I heard him gasp. "Shot? But...?"

"In the head," I said. "By persons unknown, while on his way to see us here at Lake Speer."

"Hold the fort," he yelled. "I'll get *that* story written and see you first thing in the morning. I can still get a plane."

"Be careful," I said dryly. "*Daily Express* men aren't very popular up here."

I hung up. I was glad Larry was coming to help straighten things up. I wasn't very sorry Oland Johnson was a corpse.

Crocket was busy in the lab. When I found a book with a decent title I went to Ann's room. I heard the tube of the *Memory Finder* as it spun in its colorful orbit in the lighted lab. Professor Crocket was working on something. Working against time.

Barney was sound asleep, snoring loudly.

I made myself comfortable in a blanket covered wicker chair, drew the light close to my head, and looked at Ann. She was already asleep, breathing softly. Her face was calm and lovely on the pillow.

"Remember, Johnny," I said to myself, "you're a perfect gentleman."

I opened the book.

MY EYELIDS came apart reluctantly as though they had been stuck with paste. I was still in the chair, or at least partly in it. The book was on the floor and the light was weak and almost invisible in the clear sunlight that streamed through the windows.

I stretched and found out that my neck, though stiff, was still connected with my shoulders.

Ann was asleep. I don't think she had moved since midnight. I stood up, stretched, and went silently to the bed. I leaned over, and feeling like a thief, kissed her gently on the forehead. She didn't move. I kissed her again, this time full on the lips. She smiled and moved in her sleep.

I went outside. In the hall, the phone caught my eye and the night's events came flooding back. At once I was conscious of a splitting headache. Perhaps I could dress and have a walk by the lake before the others awakened.

I pushed the door to my room open and stood there, staring at the bed.

I had been an idiot. *Barney Slocum was gone.*

I was frightened over what his absence meant to us all. Barney was the only man who might tell us the names of the men who were back of the fight against the *Express*. Barney, whom I had grown to trust, had pulled that "my pal" stuff on me until I thought he meant it.

Perhaps there was still a chance.

In two minutes flat I had my shoes on. I found a pair of corduroy trousers and a striped wool shirt. I hit the hall with the shirt half on and once outside ran swiftly down the trail to the lake.

In the sand I found Barney's footprints. I followed them north.

Barney must have listened to the sound of the boat, the day Crocket hid it. He wasn't half so dead to the world as we had thought. I followed the trail for a long time, knowing what I would find, or rather what I wouldn't find.

In the cove, I saw the mark on the beach where the boat had been tied. Barney's footprints were there.

Sick at heart, I retraced my footsteps toward the cottage.

Ann was awake and in the kitchen. I went in and sat down at the table.

I didn't know how to break the news.

"Morning, Johnny," she said. "Thanks for watch-dog act last night. I slept like a log."

"Barney's gone," I said.

"*What...?*" She whirled, frying pan in her hand, and stared at me. "Johnny—you don't mean...?"

I nodded. "He escaped in the night. Stole the boat."

I thought she was going to cry.

"Everything happens to us," she said. "I guess we've lost our last chance to find out who murdered Mr. Johnson."

I didn't say anything. I couldn't. I managed to put away an egg and a slice of toast.

"Hasn't Crocket awakened yet?" I asked.

She shook her head. I noticed that she didn't look at me again. She kept busy, her eyes on the stove.

"Maybe I'd better awaken him."

I stood up and went to Crocket's room. I knocked several times without an answer. At last, I opened the door and went in. He wasn't in bed. The bed hadn't been slept in.

Had Crocket pulled out also? Had he gone away like Barney, to let us face the music alone?

That wasn't like the Professor. I had grown to look at him as a father.

Then I remembered the light in the Laboratory, the whirring of the *Memory Finder*. Had anything happened...?

I ran to the laboratory door and tried it. It was locked.

"Professor?"

ONLY silence. I thought I could hear the faint hum of the electric motor. I wasn't sure. I didn't call Ann. I ran out the front door and around to the windows that looked in upon the room. Crocket was lying in the box of the *Memory Finder*. One hand was flung over the edge of the box. It was stiff and very white. A strange blue light hung like a mist over the slowly rotating tube.

I picked up the same stick of wood that I had thrown at Barney. I hit the window with all my strength and felt it go to pieces under the impact. I reached in, released the catch, and opened the glassless sash. In a second I was over the sill and into the room.

"Johnny—Johnny!"

Ann was pounding on the door. Her voice rang with fear. I ran to the door and released the catch. It flew open and she ran it. I went to the machine and snapped off the motor.

I felt Crocket's pulse. It was very faint, but he was still alive.

I knew very little of the machine and how it worked. I stood there, staring dumbly at what seemed to be a white, stiffened corpse.

Then a strange thing happened. The blue light faded, and Crocket's finger started to move, groping for the switch. He was still trying to turn off the motor, as he had evidently had been trying to do when he was overcome.

Thank heavens it wasn't too late. I took his hand in mine and started to rub his arm. Blood poured, back into it. He moved. His eyes opened, stared at me, and fluttered closed again.

A weak smile parted his lips.

"Thanks," he said, and lay still. He looked normal now, his face flushed and alive again.

I didn't tell Professor Crocket about Barney. I couldn't do it, at least not until he was fully recovered.

He sat up in bed and told us the story of the *Memory Finder*.

"You'll have to know," he said. "You should have known long ago. I realize now that if something happened to me, you'd be unable to go on alone.

"I told you the *Memory Finder* would make a man tell memories under its power. If you were under the machine's control, you would tell everything that has happened to you in any year I chose to set the machine. It isn't designed for the job we did on Barney Slocum. It works well; as we found out, but that isn't its real use." He was still very ill, and spoke in a low voice. I held Ann's hand and leaned very close to his lips.

"I'll be better soon. Then I'll show you how to do what I failed to do tonight. I told you once that our history is a bogus one. That we remember things that actually never happened. If I am able to set the machine back far enough, somewhere along the line, the person under its power will refuse to remember anything. The false memories that were placed in our minds will refuse to function and the subconscious mind will take-over."

He hesitated, and Ann pressed a cup of coffee to his lips. He sipped it.

147

"The subconscious mind will do one of two things. Either it will refuse to disclose information that doesn't truly exist, or it will skip the gap and tell us what happened before we came here—what happened on that other planet."

Ann was smiling. It wasn't completely sincere. She had grown to love Crocket as I had, but she refused, even now, to believe that we had any past but the obvious one.

"You will see, child," Crocket noticed her look of disbelief, and did not condemn her for it. "Perhaps you will prove to us that our theories are sound."

Ann squeezed his hand.

"If you promise to stay in bed and rest today," she said, "I'll be a good little guinea pig."

CHAPTER TEN
Murder Clues and Hot News

LARRY arrived at noon. He's the only man I know who can kiss Ann on the lips without making my fists tighten. He did it, too, and enjoyed the contact as any normal man might. Ann blushed like a schoolgirl and pretended to be angry. After Larry had paid Pinky Robin for the drive up to the lake, Pinky departed and Larry cornered me for the full story of Johnson's death. He had called Captain Steele and gathered enough material for the story. Steele refused to comment on his attitude toward the case.

"He's a good guy, though," Larry insisted. "You don't have to worry about him."

"I wasn't," I said. "Did the second half of my article go to press today?"

He grinned. "You know," he said thoughtfully, "you've got something there. Transworld Press asked permission to send that story to their papers. That means three-quarters of the world will read it before tomorrow night."

I wasn't unhappy about that.

"Perhaps we'll hit a few intelligent readers with that kind of circulation," I said hopefully.

Larry grimaced. "You've sold me," he admitted. "I half expect to be pulled out of this world at any minute and tossed to another planet. Don't get the idea that we aren't reaching intelligent people with the *Express*. Before I left a hundred phone calls had come in. People want to know where they can reach you and Crocket. *Life* is sending up a photographer for an essay on Crocket, and the way he lives."

I wanted to tell the Professor but he was still confined to his room.

"And that's not all," Larry said. "A certain wolf of Wall Street named Jeffery Pinchott called me. He wanted to talk to Johnson. The Johnson murder story hadn't hit the street yet. Pinchott called long distance because he was out of town. Told me to lay off your story or he'd see the *Express* burning in hell, press by press."

Pinchott? I wondered if he was one of the men behind Barney Slocum's jaunt to Lake Speer. I thought I should tell Larry Keen the whole story. I did, in the next half hour, while Ann prepared lunch and went to see how Professor Crocket felt.

We spent the afternoon bathing and talking over plans for the future, what few we had. It was close to dark before Crocket felt like getting up. The sun was setting when the roar of a car sounded on the highway.

"Probably Steele is coming up," I said. "I'm pretty sure he'll have something of interest to tell us, by this time."

Keen changed from his bathing suit into street clothes, made a call to New York, and reported that the city was buzzing over Professor Crocket and his strange story.

Then a car roared down the drive and damned near turned over as it turned on the soft grass and halted before the porch. It wasn't Steele.

A gaunt, pale faced man jumped out. He carried a black brief case and wore a velvet-collared coat and black felt hat. He threw open the, porch door and stormed in. I was the first person to stop him. I think he was determined to search every room, if necessary, to dig us out.

I looked over his shoulder and noticed a chauffeur, sitting stiffly in the car. It was an expensive model.

"Where in the hell is Crocket, or the John Sharp who licks his boots?"

The question was spoken harshly, as though he kept a piece of sandpaper in his mouth to sharpen his tongue.

It didn't exactly promote friendship on my part.

"My name is Sharp," I said. "But I'm not in the habit of cleaning boots in the manner you suggested."

HE DIDN'T offer his hand. He slammed his brief case down on the porch swing, removed his gloves and hat, and sat down beside the lease.

"My name is Pinchott," he said in an important voice. "Jeffery Pinchott of New York. I want to see this crackpot Crocket."

Professor Crocket appeared at the door.

"Then you may come into my laboratory," he said in a cool voice. "That is if you make up your mind to use a slightly more friendly method of handling your hosts."

Pinchott turned an ugly red, stood up without a word, gathered his gloves, hat, and brief case, and followed Crocket into the hall.

I heard the door to the laboratory close. I wandered out to the car and smiled at the chauffeur.

"Nice boss you got," I said.

"Nice enough to me," he said, a tiny bit of sharpness in his voice.

He wasn't the friendly type. I didn't intend to get pushed around twice in the same day. I went over and put one foot on the running board. I was on the right hand side of the car.

"What's the matter with you two?" I asked. "Been eating snails for dinner?"

He didn't answer. He was the perfect chauffeur that you see in the movies. I took my foot off the running board and started to turn. The back window was rolled down an inch or two.

On the glass were dozens of tiny microscopic specks of dust. Otherwise the glass was clean and well polished.

I tried not to jump to conclusions. Yet, the idea seemed quite possible. I looked at the chauffeur again, but he ignored me, staring straight ahead.

I looked down at the tires. They were clean, and wet from the damp grass. Casually, I sauntered back around the car, toward the cottage. As I did so I glanced down at the left tires. They were covered with mud. The wheels were muddy half way to the hubs.

I remembered Pinky Robin's description of the murder car.

It had swerved off the road on the left hand side and the shot had been fired through the rear window.

Were the spots on the back window powder marks from the death gun?

I knew there was a job I had to do. In a few hours both the powder marks and the tires would be washed clean.

Captain Steele had to see them for himself before it was too late. I tried to walk slowly as I went to the cottage. I reached the phone and called police headquarters. It seemed like an hour before I contacted Steele.

I kept my voice low but there was no need for it. The conversation in the lab was pitched well above my voice.

I HAD just hung up the receiver when Big Business in the form of irate Jeffery Pinchott shot from the laboratory door, fairly ran along the hall, and stopped to face me. His lips were blue with anger. He shook from head to foot.

"You addle-brained idiot," he shouted. "I can't reason with that crack-pot."

"The name is Crocket," I corrected him.

"Don't be smart with me, young fellow," he snapped. "Will you see that those articles are properly covered by a statement that they are not the truth, and that you made an error in writing them?"

I would like to have taken a crack at him then and there. He was so damned cock-sure of himself. I knew that Steele should be on his way and I had to stall Pinchott as long as possible. I adopted a slightly more friendly attitude. I knew, also that Larry Keen was listening to every word from his place in the kitchen. Pinchott was apt to break loose with stuff Larry could use.

"Just what have you against Professor Crocket and myself?" I asked.

Pinchott, who reminded me of a buzzard about to land on his prey, calmed himself enough to speak civil English.

"For your information, I control a good share of big business in New York," he said. "I also represent men who own a large share of the *Express*. These articles are throwing the whole market to the wolves. What you've printed has knocked buying and selling in the head. Soon the whole country, perhaps even our foreign trade, will stop and wait for what's going to happen next. We can't allow such a condition to exist. It isn't healthy."

I grinned.

"You mean it stops the flow of the coin of the realm into your money boxes." I heard Steele's car on the state highway. "No, Mr. Pinchott," I said, "I'm sorry, but the story remains as it is. We'll release more material later. For the time being, you can tell your chauffeur to take the shortest route and drive you straight to hell."

He raised his brief case in his hand. For a minute I thought he was going to hit me with it. Then he thought better of the idea, turned and stormed out.

Over his shoulder, he shouted, "I'll wreck the *Express* for this. I'll buy it, lock, stock, and barrel."

Steele's car had already turned and was coming down the private road when Pinchott drove out. They would meet somewhere on the one-way stretch.

Larry came out of the kitchen. He looked worried.

"Pinchott wasn't talking through his hat," he said. "He knows who has the stock. He might be able to bully Oland Johnson's representatives into selling enough for a controlling share."

Captain Steele drove in five minutes later. He climbed out of his car. He saw me on the porch and smiled, rubbing a weary hand over his forehead.

"Mr. Pinchott is quite a character," he said. "I'm threatened with everything but the electric chair. He's going to have my job for holding him up for a witless conversation."

I had already told the others what I found out about Pinchott's car. Ann was for arresting Pinchott at once, and hanging him by the ears. Larry congratulated me for calling Steele.

"Did you find that my story checked?" I asked, as he came into the screened porch.

He nodded. "Only the power of God and the State Police kept him from driving right through me," he said dryly. "I asked him a few silly questions, about why he was there and got nasty answers. While I talked, I checked the glass and the tires. You might be right. Pinchott says he flew to Twin Cities and borrowed a friend's car for the trip up here. He said he was in New York last night."

Larry Keen interrupted. "Pardon me, Captain Steele." He stepped forward and introduced himself. "Pinchott called me last night. *He called by long distance.* I can have that checked."

"We'll do it, at once," Steele turned to me again. "Any idea how he might have managed the killing?"

I had been thinking of nothing else for the past hour.

HE KNEW Johnson was coming here, and he knew, also, that Johnson had consented to print the second article. He probably tried to reason with the owner of the *Express*, failed to do so, and followed him last night. It was rainy, but Johnson evidently hadn't rolled up the window in Pinky's car.

"Johnson was sitting on the left side of the rear seat. Pinky drove fast and took most of the road. Pinchott told His man to cut out on the left shoulder of the highway and the tires sank in the mud. They pulled up beside the car Robin was driving. Pinchott rolled his window down and took a rather lucky shot. The glass was damp and the powder stains stuck to it."

Steele nodded thoughtfully. "Pinchott is the type who would kill," he said. "He'd depend on his money and position to save him."

"We might get the chauffeur, to talk," Keen suggested.

"I'm afraid not;" I said. "He's a good mate for Pinchott. If my theory is correct, that chauffeur already has enough money to support him for the remainder of his life. Pinchott parked somewhere last night. He went to town and checked with the New York office this morning. When he found out the *Express* was already on the street, he called Keen and asked for Johnson. A nice way to establish an alibi. He overlooked the fact that we might check the call."

After that we talked everything over carefully. I felt that Steele trusted us, at least to the extent of making his investigation a quiet one. He knew nothing about Barney Slocum, and I was glad of that. It might go bad for the sentimental gunman.

Steele left after he had sampled a stack of Ann's pancakes. I told Crocket of Slocum's disappearance and he and the others agreed that we could do nothing about it. Thus, for the time being, the Johnson murder case was in Steele's hands. We hoped he could pin it on Pinchott, and do so before Pinchott was able to work the *Daily Express* deal in his favor.

"Thought, you'd like to see what's happening in your hometown," Larry said. He dropped several copies of the *Express* on my lap. "While I was at the crossroads, I called New York. They checked the Pinchott call. It came from Bradbury, a little town about thirty miles south of here. I let Steele talk with long distance. He's in touch with the police in New York and at Twin Cities. They expect to let Pinchott return to New York without disturbing him. They'll take the car and the chauffeur just as soon as he leaves his friend at Twin Cities."

All of this was good news.

"What's your personal opinion, Larry?" I asked. "Can they make Pinchott talk with the evidence they have?"

He shrugged. "I'm afraid not," he said. "Pinchott can buy lawyers and judges by the dozen. He doesn't like what the *Express* did. It's a personal grudge now against you and Crocket."

He went inside and I heard him challenge Ann to a swim. I felt bewildered. The theory of the bogus world hadn't

155

affected Ann or Larry as it had me. I was anxious to have it over with as soon as possible.

I watched them go toward the lake, then settled down with the papers. Larry had written the introduction to the second installment of "Professor Crocket's Papers."

New York—May 6. Our last Sunday edition of the Daily Express including the startling story by Reporter John Sharp telling the world about Professor James Crocket and his theory that the world is a synthetic product placed here to test man's reaction to environment. The article received such widespread attention that we are devoting the front page to the second and last installment. Although the Express refuses to comment on its own attitude toward Crocket, we are willing and anxious to present to you the full story, so that you, the reader, can draw your own conclusions."

I STARTED to read the story, wondering if I had been entirely sane the night I worked over it so carefully. A car roared on the highway. I listened and it turned down the private road. Then another came within hearing distance. In ten minutes, just as the first vehicle came skidding to a halt outside the door, I could count seven different cars on their way toward the cottage.

As Crocket was busy in the lab, and the others were swimming, I met the tall, curly headed youth that jumped from the coupe and ran in my direction. "You're Sharp of the *Express,*" he said breathlessly. "My name is Williams of the *Chicago Day.* Give me the first break, will you?"

He pumped by hand eagerly and stared back toward the highway. I was beginning to get the drift. It had always been like this. Every time something broke that would prove of nationwide interest, we reporters flocked in like farmers to a threshing. I liked Williams' look. He was young, clean-cut and at least he recognized me from my photo in the *Express.*

Grinning, I dragged him hurriedly along the hall and into the laboratory. Crocket looked up from the machine and came toward us."

"I think I'm…"

"This is Williams," I said, "a reporter from Chicago. He's the first of a long line of bums who will try to rush us for the next few days. Pull down the curtains and lock the door. Tell Williams everything you want published and don't come out until he has the whole story."

Crocket's eyes twinkled. He turned to Williams.

"It seems you've impressed Mr. Sharp," he said.

Williams was like a kid with a new train.

"Golly," he pumped my hand again, "you're all right."

"No," I disagreed. "But I was a cub reporter once. Santa Claus gave me his first interview, and I never forgot it."

I went into the hall and slammed the door. I heard Crocket slip the bolt in place. By the time I reached the front lawn, reporters were all over the place. Cameras clicked and someone howled:

"Hold it, Sharp. Let's get one as you open the porch door."

I opened the door and walked out. It was a nice feeling. This was the first time I'd been in *front* of the cameras. There were a dozen cars in the yard. *Life* had a man sitting on the roof of the cabin, getting an angle shot of the whole scene. Someone asked where Johnson was murdered. I pointed to the spot.

"Get those buggies out of line with my camera," the photographer on the roof yelled. "Pull one sedan up and open the door like it was when Johnson's body hit the dust."

"Where's the murder car?" the *Herald* man asked.

"Down at the cross roads" I said. "Ask for Pinky Robin. He'll charge you a quarter for each pic."

That was my idea, but I figured Pink could use the spending money.

Willard, of the Twin Cities *Gazette,* a man whom I had heard a great deal about approached me.

"Now that the dust has settled," he asked, "where's Crocket?"

I had been waiting for that. "I have allowed one representative to interview Professor Crocket," I said. "When he comes out he'll type his story. He's a good kid and I'm letting him phone his stuff from here. You boys will get carbons of what he has to say. You can send your stories from town. He'll have a ten-minute start on you. It's a kind of revenge I'm getting for what you all used to do to me."

Willard chuckled. "I heard you were pretty slick, Sharp," he said. "Okay, we'll wait." *Life* clambered off the roof, put away his plates, and caught me.

"I need some shots of you and Crocket together," he said. "How about some laboratory shots?"

"Crocket will be out later," I said. "Photograph him, but ask me the questions. He's a busy man."

"But the lab," *Life* protested. "I've got to…"

"Can you take pictures through a locked door?"

"Okay," he said. "Don't get hot about it."

I SPENT an hour satisfying the press about what we were doing. Then Williams came out and typed his story on the porch. He gave everyone copies of it, and God, did he feel proud. Then he made his phone call from the hall and labeled the story "Exclusive."

I imagine his editor, waiting in Chicago, chalked up a nice pay raise for the kid.

The yard cleared, with the exception of *Life*, who waited to record Crocket on film. Ann came up from the lake, looking wet and lovely. *Life* paid more attention to Ann than he did to Crocket.

(I might add that Ann, still dripping and lovely, was featured on the cover of the following week's *Life*. Crocket and I "also ran" on page forty.)

CHAPTER ELEVEN
Ann "Remembers"

IF WE thought the reporters were to be our last visitors, we were wrong. If the story I had written hit the world below the belt, the influx of tourist trade hit us in the same place. Inside of twenty-four hours Lake Speer was the most popular spot in Minnesota. I mentioned that an old camp was located at the far end of the lake. It was made up of dilapidated cottages, owned by Lake Speer farmers, and rotting with years of unuse.

Every cottage was rented. Pinky Robin became chief guide and transportation chief between the railroad station and the lake.

A tent colony was established.

I confessed that Crocket was planning certain experiments to prove his theory. By late afternoon of the following day, Captain Steele had sent up half a dozen troopers to keep an eye on the cottage. The private road was roped off and traffic on it forbidden. The lake became dotted with boats and one trooper established himself at the beach to keep them from landing.

Under the scrutiny of the world, Professor Crocket continued to work quietly in his laboratory. His light was burning all through the night. Uniformed men sat in the pines outside the windows, smoking and talking in quite respectful voices.

From the Daily Express, Thursday, May tenth— "Professor Crocket's work has rocked the world—Crocket recognized by many, as genius—markets low—no buying—world business on thread—reaction varied in different quarters—men of science gather to study and discuss Crocket's findings."

Daily Express—same day—The police here today questioned powerful Wall Street executive, Jeffery Pinchott, concerning murder of Oland Johnson. Pinchott appeared before District Attorney to be faced with photographs of the car he used when in the vicinity of Lake Speer. Powder marks—and..." The article ended, "Pinchott was released temporarily. His lawyers laugh at the charge."

Daily Express—May 11— "Pinchott case will never go, to court," lawyers say. "Pinchott's reputation is spotless. He seems in no way connected with the strange events that have been taking place at Lake Speer, Minnesota."

The story went on for a full column, rehashing Johnson's death and the *"bogus world"* theory.

Then on May twelfth, the bombshell broke right in my lap. I caught the paper Larry tossed at me as he came in from town. He stood there waiting for me to unfold it and read the headline:

JEFFERY PINCHOTT
MURDERED

It was printed in black, boldface type that jumped up at me from the front page. I almost dropped the paper. I looked up at Larry, then, before he could speak, back at the sub-head:

Jeffery Pinchott, Powerful Wall Street Magnate, Shot Through the Head Today

The story was long, but I read only the first paragraph:

New York, May 12—Jeffery Pinchott was shot through the head today, as he rested in his home after an interview with the police. A maid, Miss Janice West, who discovered the body, said she called the police at once. Upon arriving, Inspector Patrick McDonald said Jeffery died at his desk. The murder weapon has not been found. An open window beside the desk indicated the murderer's probable method of escape.

There was more. Lots more. Before I could read it, I had to find out if Larry had drawn the conclusion that I had. I stared up at him.

"That solves a lot of things, doesn't it?" he said.

I nodded. "Barney?"

He smiled. "I'd forget the name of Barney Slocum, if I were you," he said. "You told me Slocum said you 'wouldn't be sorry' the night he escaped. You also told me that he seemed to be a 'good sort of fellow.' Well, I'd say only this. Barney is a killer. He didn't like Pinchott, because Pinchott was your enemy. Maybe he did it for you. Maybe he did it for Ann or the Professor. Anyhow, it's done and it's the only way there was to bring Jeffery Pinchott to justice. The law couldn't fight his millions."

"But they'll catch Barney," I said. "Of course, we're jumping at conclusions."

He shook his head. "I don't think so. Who else would dare walk in on Pinchott like that? No, it was a good, clean fast job. That's the way Barney Slocum works."

SO THE day passed, and a couple of hundred more "campers" came to the lake. The place was a madhouse. You couldn't walk to the lake without feeling a hundred eyes on you. Ann had borrowed a typewriter from Steele's office. We converted her bedroom into an office and she was hard at work trying to sort and answer some of Crocket's flood of mail. Twice a day Pinky Robin drove up from town with a mail sack full of it.

But now I had a new interest in the mail. Somehow, sometime, I expected to receive a communication from a murderer.

May thirteen— Crocket was still in the lab. He didn't sleep at all, the night of May twelfth. I told him about Pinchott, but he seemed unimpressed. He's thankful for the police net around the cottage, as he can't stand interference now.

His only comment on Pinchott was: "Dead or alive, he couldn't stop us now. We are on the verge of a terrific discovery."

I left him alone and went into Ann's room. The typewriter was clicking a mile a minute. As I passed Larry, he was talking on the phone. He kept a direct, line open with the office and handled his work by long distance telephone.

Ann looked up when I came in. She was tired but excited.

"You should see what you two are doing to men's minds," she said, and tossed a handful of mail at me. "The world's turned upside down, and what are you going to do about it?"

I sat down opposite her and opened half a dozen envelopes.

I started to read...

"Gentlemen: "As secretary of the Gary American Legion, I must protest against the material you are causing to be printed throughout the nation. We have men in our chapter who fought in the battles of France. They came home wounded and exhausted from a war that will never be erased from their minds. Can you tell us that bullet and shrapnel scars

do not exist? Can you tell us that we dreamed that we fought a war? We demand an apology, to be printed in every paper in the world."

"Gentlemen: "I ain't so good at writing, but I'm a lifer in the State Pen at Newcastle. They got me here for murdering a guy twenty-five years ago. How in the hell could I murder a guy, if I wasn't even around here twenty-five years ago? Please do something about getting me out of here.

John Scrawbuck."

"P.S. My buddies are giving me the laugh, but they just ain't educated."

"To Crackpot Crocket:

"A bunch of us kids have got a swell Tarzan Club and we read all the Tarzan books and agree that they give us a true picture of the glorious past. We demand that you apologize to Edgar Rice Burroughs for saying that there wasn't any Tarzan and that there wasn't anything on earth when Tarzan went around in the trees and rescued pretty girls in sarongs.

"P. S. We don't care about the pretty girls, but we all took a vote and we agree that you're all wrong about Tarzan."

I READ a last letter from a refugee in New York. He wrote poor English, but his idea was sound:

"Why don't you tell Stalin it ain't worth fighting for? Maybe he'll quit."

There was a touch of humor in these letters, but I didn't see them. I saw only the little people of the world, fighting for something they all believed in. Their arguments were sound, so far as they knew. Everyone was angry.

We had to do something to prove to them that they were wrong, and at the same time give them a world worth fighting for.

"They're all like that," Ann said, when I finished. "Thousands of them. I keep writing. "Wait—we'll prove to you that we are right.""

"We will," I said, and stood up. Pinky was coming in with another bag of letters.

Ann looked distressed.

"Johnny," she touched my hand. *"Can you?"*

I had tried to make her believe. I had failed.

"Wait," I said, "until Crocket's ready. He's devoted his life and sacrificed his reputation on this thing. He's sincere, and brilliant."

She sighed. "I only hope he's intelligent enough to get you out of this mess and leave something for me when it's all over." I guess I knew how she felt. I had given up a good job and pushed our marriage date into a hazy future. Ann had proven that I was the thing she wanted most of all. I hadn't been very considerate of her.

"Pinky came in and tossed the bag on the floor.

"Good Lord," he said, and mopped his face with his shirtsleeve. "I never figured on being a mail-man. I'm getting rich off you folks. Collected a hundred bucks in carfare and tips since yesterday.

"What's going on down at the camp?" I asked.

He whistled. "About a thousand people are meeting and talking about you people," he said. "Some of them are curious. Some of them want to know what's going on and are getting damned mad because they don't find out anything."

He looked sheepish.

"Anything for my bulletin service?"

I said, "What?"

He stammered. "Bulletin service. I've made up a mimeograph sheet telling everything I find out up here. I sell it at a quarter a copy at the camp."

Pinky, I decided, was no dunce.

"You can say that we are handling letters with great dispatch, that Professor Crocket will have something definite to report within the next week and that the police have already arrested three people who tried to break through the lines."

Ann looked as surprised as Pinky did.

"Is that a fact?" he asked.

"No, it isn't," I admitted. "But it will probably keep them away. They don't want to go to jail and miss anything that might happen."

After Pinky had gone, I went down to the lakefront. Boats, dozens of them, floated lazily out by the diving raft. Some of the people in them were mere curiosity seekers. Others wore good clothing and appeared to be uncomfortable enough to be the "higher-ups" of the social world.

It was sort of a flagpole-sitting act, in boats, each contestant waiting to view the mysterious happenings at the cottage.

I had told Pinky that Crocket would soon have something to report. God protect us, if he didn't.

"N.Y. May Fifteenth— A meeting of the World Congress of Science last night voted to send a group of five representatives to interview Professor Crocket. Though doubtful that the man is more than a police protected maniac, scientists admit that his theory is interesting enough to demand immediate investigation."

I was reading aloud, at the dinner table. Steele was there and Larry, Ann, the Professor, and myself. Crocket looked tired. He hadn't slept for three nights. He listened gravely.

"I think we'll prove a match for them," he said, when I had finished. "We'll try the first step of the experiment tonight, if Ann is still willing to go through with it."

Ann, it proved, was so darned tired of the whole, thing that she would do anything to prove or disprove the theory, once and for all. It was decided that we would enter the laboratory at eight o'clock. Steele promised that extra men would be on duty. Steele, I believe had grown as interested in the experiment as any of us. He obtained Crocket's permission to be present at the, time.

Steele had been temporarily stymied by the Johnson case. His men were working on every clue. The tire marks in the mud, which Pinky pointed out, checked with Pinchott's borrowed car. Although he was unable to close the case completely, he was firmly convinced that Pinchott's death had solved the murder.

"And Pinchott is in the hands of the Devil and the New York police, so that part of the crime is settled."

I found a letter from Barney while going through the afternoon mail—unsigned. It was written on a plain sheet of paper and the envelope was date-stamped in New York.

I guess you don't have to worry about Pinchott anymore. If you ever get a crack at that other planet, and decide to take the trip, let me know. You can reach me through a personal in the Express.

signed—
The Guy you bashed in the face.

Professor Crocket came into the laboratory. He carried a large pitcher of ice water, which he placed on the table near the *Memory Finder*. Captain Steele was frankly curious about the machine, as he had been told nothing, and had picked up little information at the dinner table. Of course, I had previously explained the theory of the machine to Larry. Ann not only knew what the machine could do, but was waiting anxiously to prove that the Professor was all wrong in his thought sequence.

"Because," she explained, "you simply cannot convince me that this world didn't start in a crawly, oozy stage and gradually work up to its present power."

I was worried about placing Ann at the mercy of the machine, in spite of the Professor's promise that no harm would come to her. I remembered what had happened to him, and hoped that nothing would slip during the first carefully planned experiment.

He thought it best to explain to Ann just what would happen.

"You will feel a drowsiness coming over you. Don't be frightened. Go to sleep relaxed and don't try to fight the power of the *Finder*. You will be conscious of talking of everyday things. You'll feel an urge surging through you to tell anything that comes to mind. That part of the experiment affects the forward part of your brain.

"If, when we have placed you under full power of the machine, you want to talk, and yet can think of nothing to say, don't fight to go on. Simply relax. You won't know when your subconscious mind takes over. You won't remember a word that you repeat."

Ann was rather light hearted tonight. First, I know that being human, she felt proud of herself for being the center of attraction for so many men. Secondly, Ann thought that now she would prove to us that we were on the wrong track. That we would take our medicine, admit that we were wrong, and return to normal life. That meant a lot to her. I could see it in the misty look she gave me as the Professor assisted her into the box.

IT GAVE me a start to see her lying there, still and a little pale. She was determined but uncertainty crept into her expression and remained there, unspoken.

Crocket placed the metal bands on her wrists and on her right ankle. He attached the wires to the machine.

"I am not trying any hair-brained scheme," he said, mostly for Steele's benefit. "I've used the machine before, but never on another person. Last night I tried to go too far. Even my brain, which is more easily controlled because of long training, could not stand the strain I placed on it. I'll take no such chances with Ann."

Steele ran his finger around the inside of his collar and cleared his throat. He knew that, in his position, if anything serious happened, he would be held responsible. However, Steele was curious. He recognized in Crocket the touch of a genius.

"I'm just a bystander," he said. "I'll be glad to see this cleared up, once and for all, regardless of what decision you come to. Perhaps we can get some peace from this flock of human locusts who have swept down on the neighborhood."

The Professor nodded. He smiled. "I have more friends than I ever hoped for," he said, "thanks to the intelligent handling of my papers by Johnny."

Larry Keen stood just inside, the lab door. Steele crossed and stood by the window. Ann moved in the box.

"Please hurry," she begged. "I may change my mind if you don't."

The lab was very warm. The curtains were drawn. Crocket turned the switch and the emerald tube started to quiver, turned over, and gained speed. Ann closed her eyes. Her lips were pressed tightly together. I reached down and touched her fingers. She took my hand in hers and held on tightly.

"I'm sleepy," she said, and her hand relaxed, falling from mine.

The tube spun crazily now, and the emerald liquid faded and turned several colors in quick succession. The halo of blue appeared over the tube and Professor Crocket switched the dial until it pointed to 1942.

Ann's voice was low but strong. "I met Johnny this spring. He's the sweetest…"

I felt the blood mounting to my face and Crocket switched the dial-to 1941.

"New York is cold this spring," Ann said. "Think I'll take a few days off and try Florida."

1940—1939—back—back.

Crocket switched the dial swiftly, getting only a short sentence on each year, to convince himself that Ann actually remembered. The room was getting hot. Steele wiped the perspiration from his face. His expression was tense. I looked at Larry. A smile played around his lips.

1931—1930—

Ann's voice was still clear, though it was obvious that she was in a deep sleep. Her entire body was relaxed. Every time Crocket moved the dial, words came readily to her lips. She spoke of little, unimportant things that are important only at the time they happen. Crocket was very busy every second. He hovered over the machine and watched the light changes that came. A deep purple halo quivered above the whirling tube. Liquid swished rapidly from end to end, and the motor was hot, humming loudly.

1929—1928—

"Guess I *will* have to take higher math at school," Ann's lips said. "I love the work. Dad says I can go to New York if I pass."

Crocket's fingers were on her pulse. He looked first at me, then at Steele.

"No danger," he said coolly. "She's perfectly normal."

He switched the dial back once more. "1927 is my big year," Ann said. "I have my first party dress. It's very pretty…"

ANN would have been eight years old then. She's twenty-five now, having been born in 1919. Her memory was vague, as a child's memory usually is. She talked of her school experiences. Her excellent marks in grade school art. Then, back to 1926-1925.

She hesitated, then blurted out, "Mommy, I can't remember…yes…I'm six years old today. The cake is pretty—six green candles."

Crocket took a long breath. He switched the dial to 1925.

Ann's lips' moved. No sound came from them. Beads of perspiration moistened her face. She seemed to be struggling for words.

A five-year-old girl should remember—something.

Crocket ignored the others. He looked straight at me. There was a triumphant smile on his face. I heard Steele leave his place by the window and move slowly, silently toward me. Larry's hand was on my shoulder.

Ann's body stiffened. She was trying—trying to remember something. Anything that occurred in 1925.

"A world that has only existed twenty years," Crocket whispered, "cannot supply memories beyond that time." This was our first link of proof, and yet it frightened me. I stared down at Ann's still, almost lifeless body.

"I—I don't know," my voice faltered. "Perhaps she really can't remember. She was very young."

"No," Crocket said. "You can all remember little things that happened before you went to school."

Steele's voice interrupted. "I can remember quite clearly," he said, "my first boots—age four."

Crocket turned up the power. The motor hummed louder and the tube spun faster. Ann's body went rigid.

Crocket's voice sounded uncertain, as though he didn't quite dare "I don't know how much power she can take," he said.

"Ann was quite rigid now. I remembered Crocket's lifeless hand on the edge of the box.

"I think she's had enough," I said.

Crocket leaned close to Ann's lips. "No memories," he said gently. "Nothing—nothing about Mother or Daddy?"

Ann's head moved ever so slightly from side to side. Her mouth opened but no sound escaped.

"It still doesn't prove anything," Larry Keen said. I had the feeling that he was trying to convince *himself* that it didn't. It wasn't what he really believed.

I turned to Larry. It was a long chance. "You knew her when she first came to New York," I said. "Didn't she ever mention any childhood incidents?"

The others turned hopeful eyes on him. Larry struggled with his own memory. Then his face turned red.

"Good Lord," he said softly, "as a matter of fact she did. She used to tell me quite often of her Grandparents. It seems they had a dairy farm in Northern New York. She lived there between the ages of three and five. She could remember the impression her Grandfather's huge herd of cattle made on her."

Crocket bent over the box. "Ann," he said gently, "Ann."

Ann's fingers moved.

"Ann you remember your Grandfather's farm? All the cattle. A big farm where you lived."

Silence—dead, intolerable silence hung over the room like a foggy curtain.

"No farm," she said quite distinctly. "No Granddad—no farm." She sighed, as though giving the whole thing up for a bad job. *"No nothing."*

CROCKET sprang the motor switch. He cut the power and the tube slowed to a stop. My eyes were on Ann's face. To my relief, her eyes opened. Color flowed back into her face. She started to get up.

"Just a minute," Crocket said. "Do you remember an incident that you mentioned when you were asleep? Something about enjoying the company of your grandparents? Living with them and being impressed by their herd of dairy cattle?"

Ann smiled. "I do have a memory for the oddest things," she said unsuspectingly. "Remember, Larry, my telling you all about Grandfather Wiggins and his big farm?"

Larry nodded. He couldn't trust himself to speak.

Crocket released her from the ankle and wristbands. He helped her out of the box and she gave me a pleased smile.

"I hope that proves something, once and for all," she said.

Crocket chuckled happily. "It proves," he said, "that you didn't remember any such thing as a farm. Larry told us about it and we tried to help you along. Ann, my dear, by your own confession, nothing happened to you before 1925. As you expressed it, 'no Granddad—no farm.'"

Ann turned to me. Her eyes swept around the room at Steele, and at Larry Keen. The blood left her face and she nearly fainted.

"I thought we'd need the ice water," Crocket said, and reached quickly for the pitcher.

CHAPTER TWELVE
Barney Slocum Dies for Fifty Grand

STEELE insisted upon going under the machine the same night.

"Because," he said, "one test won't be enough. You'll have to test every screwball that comes along, and get the President himself to sign a paper stating that you're not crazy. Others will refuse to believe."

Crocket was overjoyed at Steele's proposal. He had anticipated Steele's argument against the use of the machine, and now that Steele was on our side, it would help a great deal to convince others.

He tested Steele's memory. Steele mentioned his police work, and talked a great deal about his schooling. As in Ann's case, Steele's mind became a blank when the dial was set on 1925. Even Larry, hard-hearted editor that he was, seemed visibly impressed this time. The working conditions were much the same. The room had grown much warmer and Steele ceased to struggle, his subconscious mind telling him that it was useless to try when Ann had failed.

But it was Steele that enabled us to clear up much of the mystery. Even Crocket refuses to attempt to explain, though it's something that has troubled us since that night.

We were about to turn off the machine, to return Dan Steele to normal, when a strange, thing happened.

His lips did not move. His mouth was open and a strange hollow voice came from his throat.

"Wait—I, Xerbes claim that it can be done."

Ann, standing tensely at my side, pressed closer, her nails cutting into my arm. Larry Keen was so startled that he jumped backward, almost falling. I looked at Crocket. His eyes were lost in a mass of wrinkles. His fists were clenched.

"Good Lord," the words were breathed softly. He sprang to Steele's side. The Captain was rigid. His body seemed a dead, white thing. Yet the voice came from his mouth again, echoing and pounding against the walls of the little room. It was a voice from a huge soundbox. It was as though it came from a vast cathedral.

"The experiment may sound fantastic," it said, "yet Yanu and the High Scientists will find a way."

Up to this point, I had felt as though the inner brain was speaking. Now this theory was lost, because another voice came. *A voice entirely different than the first.* It echoed, as did the voice that called itself Xerbes. Yet it was different in tone quality.

"And I, Unar, claim it cannot be done. Man will not conquer his environment. The planet of Moneta is a complete world. We have lived here from the 'O' age. We live by the things that we found here, developing only as those first blessings are developed and improved."

Then the first voice again:

"We will make a wager. We will prove that you are wrong. The High Scientists, under my leadership, will construct a false world. It will be enlarged by the machinery at our control and thrust into space. On this world we will construct ruins. They will be buried at several levels. In addition, there will be books, *ersatz* materials, in fact, enough bogus history to intrigue the minds of those who go there."

"Wait," the voice of Unar interrupted. "What of the people? They will retain memories of Moneta."

I looked at Crocket. He was torn between duty and curiosity. We all knew that Steele might be dead. Perhaps this was the very voice of death. Yet, none of us moved. *We could not move.*

"No," Xerbes thundered. "I will not lose this wager by forgetting important things. Each human who is set down on this eratz world will be put under one of our Memory Machines. All memory of Moneta will be wiped out. Into each mind will be placed a complete, personal history. Books, even living quarters, will be constructed to dovetail with these memories."

Another voice came in, as though we were listening to a strange radio play. A radio program came from the white, motionless lips of a seemingly dead man.

AND Xerbes and I claim that these people, at least a percentage of them, will be intelligent enough to discard the hopeless jigsaw puzzle of history that we place about them. These higher ones will understand, when they have wasted many years in study, *that no one can completely solve the mysteries of such a world.* They will struggle through mists of uncertainty and find their way back to Moneta *and their rightful home.*"

A great volume of voices arose, some of them cheering, some defiant.

"This is a mad, foolish scheme you have concocted," Unar's voice boomed.

"But," Xerbes cried, "you, Unar, claim that we are bound by environment. That we live according to the conditions about us. I say that we can master environment and ignore it. That we can rise above it. I say that the people of this false world we create will realize that their past does not make sense. That they will muddle through and come home to us, and I will collect the wager."

At this point, Steele's lips started to twitch convulsively. His body stiffened. Frightened, I jumped forward and turned the switch of the machine. It went dead. Crocket and Larry were at Steele's side.

For a moment I thought we were too late. Then Steele relaxed once more and blood found its place in his cheeks. He opened his eyes.

"I'm—I'm thirsty as hell," he said. "Jeez."

His voice died, but his breathing, his pulse, were normal.

In five minutes he was out of the box and able to be moved, with my help, to the porch. The others came out one by one, and silently took their places in the porch chairs. Ann was silent. Larry Keen kept muttering to himself.

"Well," Steele asked. "I hope I didn't disappoint you?"

Ann sighed. "You—you knocked my performance right off the first page," she said.

Steele looked first at me, then at Crocket.

"I had no memories beyond 1925?"

Crocket shook his head. He seemed to be in a daze. He had never expected anything like the performance of the *Memory Finder*.

"Good Lord, man," he said, breathlessly, "you acted like a human radio. As near as I can guess, you tapped a knowledge of the past that no man has a right to know. I don't know if it was you or the machine."

Eagerly he told Steele what had happened. When he was finished, he sat very still. The moon was high over the lake. Boats were still out there on the lake, half a dozen of them. A couple of troopers were playing cards under the gleam of a flashlight on the lawn. It was a very quiet night. A very warm one.

"I guess you turned out to be a prophet after all," Steele said finally. "But how in the devil can we contact this Moneta that we are supposed to return to?"

Crocket shook his head. "The work has only begun," he said. "We'll have to convince others that we are right. That, alone, is a huge task. Yet I think it can be done."

"Amen," Larry Keen said. "So help me, I'll publish every word of what has happened. God pity me when the public gets hold of *this* news."

I looked at the troopers, enjoying their game of gin rummy.

"A lot of people are in for a rude awakening," I said.

"Maybe," Ann said timidly, "we'd better travel a little further on the road to Moneta before we try to convince the public that such a road exists." Ann was right but I knew I had come a long way toward success in convincing *her*.

THE full story of the *Memory Finder* was printed in the *Express*. To my surprise, I now found that although the Johnson estate hadn't been cleared up as yet, Larry Keen and several of his associates owned a controlling share in the paper. Keen had accumulated stock over a period of years, and at least for the present, he was in full charge of the paper's policy.

I kept notes from this point on, because I realized that what was happening would make a startling journal, once Professor Crocket succeeded in closing the last chapter of his story. As some of the events that took place are slightly hazy now, in view of what has happened since, I present them as I wrote them during those seven wild days that followed:

MAY 20— By noon on the day the *Express* carried its third great story of Professor James Crocket's work, Lake Speer became a maddened beehive of humanity. Steele had to rush down to State Headquarters and requisition extra troopers to keep order. I rose early and Crocket and I held a hurried conference in my room. Ann's typewriter was already clicking, trying to dig its way down through the huge pile of letters.

Crocket is looking older, tired and yet more sure of himself than ever.

"We have convinced a few intelligent people. Our work has ceased to be a theory, and is a fact," he said. "Now—we must actually develop a machine that will transport some of us to Moneta."

Moneta. The name was rich, musical. I never doubted that the planet of Moneta existed. Xerbes—Yanu—Unar—the voices that came from Steele's lips, were real living people.

"I'm still a little dazed about last night," I admitted. "We've come across something that's too hot to handle, and yet we can't stop now. There isn't any trail back—"

Crocket nodded. "That's it exactly," he agreed. "To admit that we were dreaming up the facts that we've given the public, would brand us both as fools. We have a choice of being fools, or perhaps, prophets without honor. Are you going on with me? It's not too late for you to get out."

That brought a smile to my lips. Get out? He couldn't get rid of me now no matter how hard he tried.

"The voices mentioned that we would find our way back home to Moneta. They must have given us some clue."

Crocket, nodded. "They did," he said. "I told you once this had been my life's work. It took ten years to perfect the *Memory Finder.* I managed to do something with it that I thought was impossible. Don't think that I thought only of contacting the planet called Moneta. I knew I would have to go there, if such a road opened for me. I have an attachment that fits on the *Finder.* I have used it often to carry brain waves out of my body to distant points."

"Wait a minute," I begged. "I'm a reporter. That sounds pretty complicated."

Crocket smiled. "Any task is complicated to a man who does not know how to perform it. Remember that I have worked on this for many years. The brain waves or thought waves can do everything but actually see. They have to see by sense of vibration. In a state of coma I have been able to send all but the actual brain substance to any given point. When I awaken, I have filed away in my head certain events that my brain waves have seen or picked up at that distant point. *With enough money I would be able to go further. I would be able to actually send the brain itself and perhaps the entire physical body.*"

That is the wall that we have run into. Enough money? How much? Crocket estimates twenty five thousand dollars.

I HAVE talked with Keen. He flew to New York this morning and got back late this evening. I asked him if he knew any rich *angel* that might back us. Seated at the table with half a cup of coffee in his hand, he grinned wryly.

"I know a number that might *hang* you," he said. "The big boys are after your neck, and Crocket's, for that-matter. They are trying to suppress any news from here. They've succeeded in buying the *Herald*, but I won't sell the freedom of the *Express*.

"New York, in fact, the whole outside world, is sitting on the fence. Everyone is afraid that if Crocket *should* turn out to be correct, the old world would topple like Humpty Dumpty and break into a thousand pieces.

"The stock market, food prices, everything is way off. Everyone is waiting for Crocket to kill himself or get taken to an asylum. Still there's just enough sense in his story to make them wonder."

This was very discouraging.

"What's the news so far as a general reaction is concerned?" I asked.

He pushed a copy of the *Express* toward, me.

The headlines hit me in the face.

PROFESSOR CLAIMS CONTACT
ESTABLISHED WITH MYSTERIOUS PLANET

New York, May 20—From Lake Speer today came the report that in the presence of reliable witnesses Professor James Crocket succeeded in...

The article covered most of the front page. The only other story that broke in was a review of what had been done to date to apprehend Jeffery Pinchott's murderer. It took up a half column, offering fifty thousand dollars in cash for the murderer, dead or alive. Valuable clues had been found and the police were expecting results within forty-eight hours. Pinchott's money, I decided, was still powerful enough to wage a battle in the favor of justice. Just where the justice in this case was, I wondered.

"The World Congress of Science has met in London," Larry interrupted. "They are flying a committee here by clipper. They'll demand a hearing with Crocket the day after tomorrow."

"That was valuable news. Perhaps they would stand behind us. Larry dashed this thought to pieces.

"I might add," he said, "that those boys are ready to believe anything but the truth. It's like trying to find a cure for the head cold. No one has ever done it, and they wouldn't believe it if it happened."

May 20—the day closed with no further news from outside. Down at the camp, a group of sightseers spent the evening in a community sing. Troopers were getting fed up on gin rummy and had switched to poker. Ann worked late on her mail and I went to bed. I had a headache that aspirin wouldn't cure.

May 21— It happened today. Tragedy, and a perfect solution for Crocket's problem. In the eyes of the public, I'm a hero. In my own mind, I'm still doubtful as to whether it was worth it. I had no choice. Fate played me in on her hand, and I came home with the chips.

I went swimming early this morning, hoping to escape the thrill seekers who were now practically living in their boats. Yesterday's paper created quite a stir at the camp, and Pinky Robin sold out all the copies of the *Express* he could find in town at a dollar a copy.

As a result of this I had to give up the swimming idea. I didn't want to go back to the cottage. There were a lot of things on my mind that needed pondering over. I walked along the beach, then into the woods away from the direction of the camp, hoping I could escape anyone who might have seen me leave the cottage.

I had reached the cove where Barney Slocum found his boat. It was warm and the trees swept close to the water's edge, forming a screen to hide me from the lake. I sat down on a log and stared into the water. I thought I heard a gunshot far away on the other side of the lake. It troubled me for five minutes. Then I forgot it and dozed. Suddenly the roar of a motor sounded over the calm lake. I hadn't heard a motor for some time. The sightseers used rowboats.

I sat up, scanning the water trying to discover the source of the sound. Then I knew why the motor had startled me.

It was Barney Slocum's boat.

IN THE flashing sun, I saw it slip into open water, gain speed, and come hurtling directly toward me. Two more gunshots sounded faintly in its Wake, then only the motor could be heard. I was about to get out of sight. The man in the boat stood up. He was steering with one hand.

It was Barney Slocum.

I couldn't be wrong. I remembered the first time I had seen him standing in a speedboat, guiding it with one hand. He was cocky and very sure of himself.

The boat was already half way across. Then another craft came into sight. It was smaller but evidently propelled by a heavy motor for it gained slowly, cutting down the distance between the two.

I waited. Slocum drove the speedboat straight for the shore. Fifty feet out he cut the motor and got ready to jump.

I had the wild idea that he was trying to get to the cottage. That he felt his safety depended on his reaching us.

I could see his features clearly now. There was blood on his dark face, but he was grinning. He wiped the blood away and as the prow of the boat hit the sand he jumped. He fell, got to his feet quickly, and then saw me. The grin widened and he laughed aloud.

"Johnny," he said, "my God, this *is* a welcome surprise."

The other boat was half way across the lake. It was aimed like a bullet straight toward the cove. I could see two figures in it.

They were Troopers.

Barney's face had been creased badly by a bullet.

"You shouldn't have come back," I said.

He just stood there laughing. Yet, he was gauging the speed of his pursuers carefully.

"Crocket needs some dough for that last job he's got to do, don't he?" Barney's voice was calm now. It was insane, the way he stood there, watching the Troopers as they came closer.

"Get the hell out of here," I begged. "I'll tell them you aimed a gun at me and kept on running. Hide in my room at the cottage. I'll think of something."

He grinned.

"Nice going, Johnny," he said, "but you don't think these boys could catch me if I didn't want to be caught?"

His voice was scornful.

"I don't understand," I confessed.

"You and Crocket—and Ann were pretty nice to me," he said. "You've been the only decent people I ever met. There's fifty thousand bucks waiting for the guy who brings me in, *dead or alive*."

The whole plan was beginning to seep through my brain.

"Barney, for God's sake? You didn't...?"

The Troopers were almost in now. They had cut their motor and were drifting.

They couldn't see us in the protecting screen of trees. They were standing low in the boat, pistols drawn.

"This guy Pinchott was a bum," Barney said coldly, "even if he has got money. You guys ain't bums. You done something for me. Maybe this is a chance for me to do something big too."

It wasn't a time for heroics. I grabbed him by the arm and pushed.

"Run," I said. I felt choked up and sick inside. "They'll shoot you down. Barney, run, for heaven's sake."

He jerked away from me.

"I'm all done running," he said grimly. "I ran all the way from New York, just to beat the law up here."

His face was gray and expressionless. He was very tired.

"You ain't gonna spoil things now. I ain't just thinking of you. I'm thinking of Ann and the Professor. He deserves a break."

ONE of the Troopers shouted from the boat. I thought I recognized Dave Walters' voice.

"Come down to the beach with your hands up, Slocum," he yelled. "We're landing."

Slocum shot me a last desperate look.

"Play ball, Johnny, like I want it."

I swallowed. "For Crocket's sake," I said, "and Ann's."

183

A ragged smile showed his white teeth. "Good boy," he said softly and pulled a pistol from an armpit holster. Before I knew, what he had done, he whipped up the barrel of the gun and fired directly through his own heart. He sank to the grass without a sound.

The boat hit the beach and Dave Walters jumped out. Hardly knowing what I was doing I picked up the gun. I held it loosely in my hand. Dave Walters ran toward me, stopping short as he saw Barney's body before me on the sand. He whistled.

"Looks like you hit the jackpot," he said, "and with me so close to making some real dough."

His companion came up on the bank, bent down, and turned Barney's body over. I let them take the gun from my hand.

"Nice job, Mr. Sharp," Walters said. "He was a tough baby."

I looked down at Barney. The smile was still on his lips.

Play ball, Johnny, like I want it. For Crocket's sake—and, Ann's."

I remembered what he said, the "tough boy" who had come all the way from New York to deliver fifty thousand to his friends.

"Yeah," I said. "I guess he was tough all right. I couldn't miss. He was right on top of me before I fired."

I hated like the very devil to say it. I guess it was what Barney wanted.

CHAPTER THIRTEEN
The Final Plan

MAY 22— We made the preparations to receive five members of the World Congress of Science. Steele telephoned at ten this morning to tell me a check was on his desk for the sum of fifty thousand dollars. I had already explained to Ann, Larry, and the Professor what had happened on the beach. We were all sick about it, and yet, I wanted to erect a monument telling the world what the "tough guy" had done because a few people treated him squarely.

Crocket had to sidetrack further work and prepare to receive our guests. Even the airline people were impressed at the importance of these men of science who had winged their way from half way across the world to visit Lake Speer. At one in the afternoon, Steele sent out boats to clear the lake. The beach near the camp was black with people studying the sky for the first sight of the special seaplane that was coming directly from ship's side in New York Harbor.

At one fifteen a speck disturbed the sky toward the South East and the large plane came down to squat like a sitting duck on the water of Lake Speer. A cordon of Troopers escorted the men to the cottage.

It's impressive to see such men. All five of them were well into the later years of their life. One cannot blame them for being disturbed over what they had come to witness. They had spent their lives building up a series of facts that threatened to be torn down over night.

Naturally, to us, their lifetimes weren't so important. Those who had been in the laboratory the night of Steele's brain test, realized that these were actually men of Moneta and had not, as they supposed, life residence on Earth.

The names of Farley, Freamont, Bruck, Waterman, and Wells conjure up pictures of great books of learning. The men themselves were quiet, and I think, a little amazed at the great crowds that hovered nearby, many of them already firmly convinced that Professor Crocket was correct.

I will always regret that I was unable to be present for those tests. I learned afterward that Crocket was asked to work with them alone and allow no outsider, to comment on what took place behind the doors of the laboratory. Crocket, however, told me what I didn't already know, after they emerged from the laboratory late that evening, and with grim, almost frightened expressions, embarked for the return trip.

One by one they had undergone the test, all in their turn, listening and watching for the results upon his associates.

Not one of them, powerful, stubborn fact finders who tested and retested every inch of the ground, could remember a single incident of their lives beyond the year 1925.

I came across Ann, seated on the beach, staring at the lonely moonlit water. She turned as I approached and her eyes glistened. I knew that she had been crying. I sat down and placed an arm around her waist. "Tired?"

I knew she hated people who cried, and I didn't want her to guess that I knew.

She nodded. "I guess so. There's so much happening. Barney's death—and all."

"I know," I said. "I feel somehow that there's blood on my hands."

She shook her head. For some time we sat there. It grew cold and I suggested we go in. Suddenly she was clinging to me, her tear stained cheek pressed to mine. There was something frightening in the desperate way she held me.

"Johnny—how is it all going to end? It wasn't your fault, about Barney. *He wanted it that way.* If Barney believed so much in the Professor, and you believe, it *has* to be true, all of it."

"I know," I said. "I told the Professor we couldn't turn back. I hope you feel that way."

She stared up at me, and I kissed her. "I wouldn't have you quit for anything," she said. "But if we can't straighten things out in a little while, the whole world will be hiding from itself. People will go crazy."

I thought of the check for fifty-thousand dollars, lying under a paperweight on Captain Steele's desk.

"Barney donated his life for this," I said. "Tomorrow I'm going to get the money and work my damned head off until we finish."

She laughed, a little wildly.

"To think that as much as Jeffery Pinchott hated us, it is his money that works to prove that we are right."

EVERYTHING seemed a little crazy. I took her to her room and then, noticing the light was on in the laboratory, knocked softly. Crocket's voice came from beyond the door.

"Go to bed, Johnny," he said. "There's work to be done here. Work you can't help me with. You've done your part today. Get some rest, and we'll start all over again in the morning."

"Thanks," I said. "Better call it off yourself. You've been under a strain."

"In a short time," he promised. "One or two more things…" His voice trailed off.

Minutes later I undressed quietly and crawled into bed. Every muscle in my body ached. I thought of the seaplane roaring away with five men who would deliver judgment on our very existence. Perhaps they would study the whole thing among themselves and decide that Crocket was only a clever fraud. It wasn't a pleasant thought.

I woke up once close to four in the morning. A shaft of light still touched the pines outside my window. Crocket was still at work in the laboratory.

May 23— The week ended, and for me, the last day started at noon. I didn't open my eyes until eleven this morning, and then cursed myself for sleeping so late when

Professor Crocket had worked throughout the night. I went at once to the laboratory, and asked him to stop and get some sleep. He looked very bad. His face was drawn and pale. His hands were impregnated with dirt and he showed signs of collapse. He tried to laugh at me for worrying about him.

"I've assembled some of my machine," he said happily. "Now I must make a list of needed materials and you will have to fly to Chicago for them. I've already called the supply houses and asked for the assistance you need."

I called town and arranged for a private plane. At breakfast I noticed that Ann felt much better. A night's rest had done her good.

"Larry left this morning," she said. "He's returning tomorrow, after he finds out how the World Congress of Science reacts to the visit here. He thinks he should supervise the editorial handling of their story."

I was glad of that because Larry would give the news every possible break, unless it was too bad for even him to touch up. I received a long list of equipment from Crocket and asked Ann to see that he went to bed at once.

She promised and I'll admit that at her suggestion, Crocket went to his room like an obedient child. He had lived alone for so long, he thought of Ann as a daughter and a very wonderful one at that.

I waited for Pinky Robin to pick me up and we drove directly to Steele's office. I received the check. I still didn't want to take it, but I understood what the money meant to us and tried to ignore my personal emotions.

The plane was waiting for me at Speer and the flight to Chicago was a fast one.

The job Crocket put in my hands was important. I had to contact and place orders for immediate delivery with, three chemical companies, a radio supply house and several wholesale houses. I had dinner at the Blackhawk, forgot for a few minutes that I was living in a world apart, and grew anxious to return to Lake Speer.

I had planned at first to stay in the Windy City overnight, but now, seeing people dance and sing once more, I wanted more than anything else to get back to Ann.

HOW can I best record the happenings of the next three Weeks? Barney Slocum's body was taken back to New York. Larry Keen purchased a decent lot for him and Barney went to rest, never to have his chance to take a trip to "that other planet" he had dreamed of.

Professor Crocket and I labored night and day over the machine in the laboratory. To me it was an intricate system of cabinets within cabinets. Parts, made to his drawings, came by plane from Chicago Radium arrived in carefully guarded containers. A full case of powerful tubes came in and were fitted into the power chambers beneath the cabinets.

I worked hard, doing the things he thought my hands were capable of. I trusted him entirely, knowing that his mind was familiar with the task at hand.

At the end of the week, the World Congress of Science came from their chambers and released stories to all parts of the globe. It must have been wonderful, that first interview with those men. I would have liked to have covered that story.

With every man, woman and child waiting for them to speak, the silence was broken. The full story of their findings was published in a dozen languages.

It is better for me to include part of the actual article. I cannot explain it, at least to my complete satisfaction.

London, May 30— The World Congress of Science has carefully studied and discussed at great length the findings of a committee that went to Lake Speer, Minnesota, to interview

Professor Crocket. It was with shocked surprise that many of us listened to their reports and agreed that something had burst upon the world of knowledge that no man had ever remotely suspected before this time.

We, as a body of human beings, cannot force down the throats of man, a story such as the one we heard, regardless of how much we believe ourselves. Let it be remembered that *in our opinion,* the following facts are true.

1. That man (and this applies to men of our profession more than any other) has been trussed and chained by his environment. That we are forced to react to the world around us.

2. That many strides into a clearer future have been frustrated by the beliefs that tie us to the past.

3. Therefore, it might be better if we could forget a past that does not help us, and work toward a perfect future.

4. That Professor Crocket has produced a miracle of clear thinking and succeeded in convincing us that he is sincere and a genius.

5. That his findings are: (A) A planet of Moneta actually exists. (B) It is the *home* planet of our people. (C) That *world* is an experiment, and that Crocket's previous explanation as to how we came here and why it can be told and how we were supplied with an inexplainable past is completely accurate and correct.

6. We cannot say that Moneta is a place that can be reached by any present manner of transportation. We believe this to be impossible. Even the location of such a planet hasn't been determined. However, Professor Crocket believes that he can produce such a machine. In respect to him, the Congress postpones any decision until his work is complete.

7. In summing up this report, the World Congress is forced to discard previous concepts of all branches of research and wait until such time as Professor James Crocket the man who is guiding the destiny of the world, hands down his final decision.

THE article, though by no means convincing everyone of its truth, did a wonderful thing for the Professor. When he read it, tears sprang to his eyes. Here, in the presence of his fellow workers, he was conceded to be a genius. It sent him back to his laboratory, struggling harder and harder to reach his goal.

There were telegrams of congratulations from all over the world. Several schools of thought sprang up. One of them was the *So-what'ers*. *"So-what?"* was hurled from millions of lips. Actually, these people were trying to comfort themselves.

"So what?" they asked. "We're getting along all right. Environment is here and we've been struggling with it for centuries. It hasn't got us down yet."

The answer was obvious in reaching it; I fell deeply in love with an imaginary vision of Moneta. Here was a planet that would see nothing but the future. Its people would have no ties with centuries past.

In Moneta, we all agreed, no man could point to history and say:

"Wars—we've always had them and we always will. It's like a machine. We go round and round."

One night, Ann, Larry, and myself were on a wild fantasy flight to Moneta. We pictured it with tall, perfect buildings of the future. Moneta, Larry said, would know nothing of depression and hatred and wars. On Moneta, with no memories, there would be no hatred to grow until it flamed into a war. There would be no soapboxes and speeches.

The things we spoke of must have been discussed in millions of homes. Some people made a joke of the whole affair.

To us there was no joke about the existence of Moneta. We fought against time and Larry Keen championed the cause by donating every page he could to the stories we released.

In June, after the World Congress convened until autumn, the big job was done. Throngs had moved in upon us gradually until only the cottage itself and the acre of ground around it could be protected by State Troopers. Campers were everywhere in the woods. They managed to sneak close to the cottage, and we could see them, staring with wide, frightened eyes at whatever movement they could detect through the cottage windows.

The laboratory was our terminal point on Earth. Now the machine was ready. We tried to decide who would first attempt a contact with the planet of Moneta.

Moneta—Even the name made poetry when you spoke it aloud. I would lie awake at night, staring at the ceiling and repeating the name over and over. I dreamed of it. The world of perfection, released from all superstitions, hate and dogma. Soaring onward with new success, because on Moneta there would be no fear of the dark—no fear born in childish minds for things not understood.

I became very sorry for us, the people of Earth. We had been made to suffer all these fears, simply because people greater than ourselves wanted to perform a large-scale experiment. Finally a cold perspiration broke out on my forehead and a terrible fear arose inside me. *What would happen if we failed in our effort to return to the perfection of Moneta, our home planet?* The thought grew in me like a festering sore. I tried to sleep, but my subconscious mind took hold of me and I lay awake living a nightmare.

Perhaps the machine would fail. Men would look at us and condemn us for frightening them. We would suffer, and in the end, be punished for not proving what we sought to prove.

Worst of all, the world would get no relief. Men would continue to search for turtle eggs and ruins. They would go on trying to solve the missing links that didn't exist. They would fight again and again for a world of peace, and finish each battle, only to await the strength to fight again.

I slept at last, but not until the sky was gray and traffic was once more moving along the road toward the camp.

THE laboratory was dominated by the huge system of black cabinets. These cabinets made up the space in which we would lie, while being transported by Crocket's complicated machine. They were each the size of a small coffin, lined with black leather, and fitted with doors that kept the oxygen from seeping in. The six boxes were welded into one, in rows of three each. Metal and rubber tubing connected them with various parts of the machine itself.

It would be impossible to explain Professor Crocket's theory on the action the machine must take. Even I, who had worked on it steadily, knew only that we would lie in the boxes and that air would come to us from tanks. When the machine gained full momentum, it was expected to break down the brain and transport it to Moneta. If Moneta held no oxygen, we would be faced with death within a matter of seconds after reaching there. That was the chance we had to take. Crocket's figures were based entirely on the art of higher mathematics and the subject was beyond my ken.

To the outmoded *Memory Finder* had been added six larger, more powerful tubes. Each of these contained a different chemical. The smallest contained radium. It was these flashing tubes, and the huge assembly of the radio equipment under the cabinets that would provide the all-moving power.

CHAPTER FOURTEEN
We Must Remain Calm

WE PLANNED a trial test. For this test Crocket insisted on making himself the guinea pig. He explained the correct method of starting the machine and building up the power until it controlled his body. This time, Ann and I were alone with him. The Captain was busy in town and Larry Keen was midway between New York and the Lake, coming for the final test. Larry had agreed to go with us to Moneta, while Steele promised to handle the machine at Lake Speer.

Crocket entered the first chamber and I posted Ann by the thick glass window that covered the end of it. Our instructions were to wait until Crocket showed some sign of leaving the chamber. None of us were quite sure how the transition would take place.

New motors had been placed in the room to drive the big machine. I threw the switch of the first and felt power lunge into it. It gathered speed quickly and the laboratory shook under the weight of it. Within the cabinet, I could see Crocket lift his arm, signaling that oxygen was reaching him, and everything was all right. The tubes started to whirl.

I threw the second switch and the high whine of the second motor blended in with the first. The tubes twisted faster, their various contents swishing from end to end. The base, on which they were mounted vibrated and shook the cottage.

Nothing had happened yet, and the machines were going at full speed. I watched Ann's face. She shook her head.

"He's still got his hand lifted," she said.

I was discouraged. Crocket and I had decided that the body would probably disappear slowly at though into a mist. That the cabinet would become empty, and must be left tightly closed until he returned.

The vari-colored rainbows lifted into the air over the whirling tubes. The regular lighting in the room was dim.

The machine had reached maximum speed, yet nothing had happened to Crocket.

His hand was still uprisen.

Discouraged, I turned off the power and waited for the machine to stop. With Ann's help, I unlocked the cabinet and pulled out the wheeled slab on which Crocket's body was lying.

The moment I did it, I realized the terrible mistake I had made.

Crocket's body was stiff and hard. The blood seemed drained from it. By Earth standards, he was dead. And I had killed him.

"Don't stop the machine until I signal you to do so," he had warned.

We both had mistaken the uprisen hand as a signal that he was dissatisfied and ready to give up.

What could we do now?

"We'll have to get him back in," Ann said in a hushed frightened voice. "Perhaps there's still a chance."

We slid the still figure back into place as swiftly as possible. While Ann closed and bolted the door, I sprang to the motor controls. It seemed hours before the motors were in motion again.

I went to Ann's side, staring at the still, marble like figure in the cabinet. No movement—no signal. Probably if life remained, I had murdered him by opening the case—or at least by shutting off the power.

I felt as though there was no hope, yet we couldn't give up. Crocket's life meant everything now.

Ten minutes passed—then fifteen—half an hour. The motors hummed loudly and the tubes were so hot that quickly changing halos of light spun wildly all over the laboratory. Gradually we were enveloped by these lights. The glass that allowed us to look in upon Crocket grew hazy and moist. Then, dimly, beyond the moisture-beaded glass, I thought I saw movement.

I strained my eyes, clutching Ann's shoulder with my fingers.

"Did you see?"

She nodded.

"His hand fell to his side."

Still I didn't dare open the box.

Five more minutes.

Then his foot, close to us, tapped gently on the glass.

I sprang to the motors and shut off the power. The lights faded and died. The moisture on the glass disappeared.

Ann opened the cabinet. She was crying; the tears stained her cheeks—tears born of sheer relief. I know, for even if I had not been able to cry, I felt like it as we wheeled the slab out of the cabinet and helped Crocket to his feet

"I've been to Moneta" He was quite overcome. *"Johnny do you hear me? I've been to Moneta. For a while I couldn't seem to return at will. Then I was able to come back."*

"I told him quickly about turning off the machine.

"I'm glad you did it," he said. "I found that I was able to move about with complete freedom on Moneta for a short time. That means that we must have a reliable person at the controls here. By a prearranged signal, we can come back after making a study of life on Moneta. *It's wonderful."*

I was frightened. He spoke of being able to move about in complete freedom.

"Your body didn't leave the case," I said. "You grew stiff and dead from all surface evidence."

I expected this to trouble him but he chuckled.

"I should have told you," he explained. "These bodies we are in are quite useless to us. Only our subconscious minds and our souls are transported by the machine. That is why the cabinets are constructed so carefully. They must protect and preserve the actual body so that we may come back here long enough to finish our work. On Moneta science is far enough advanced to provide us with new bodies.

"I didn't have time to present myself to the people of our home planet. I found myself on a hill near the edge of a great highway. In a distance the towering spires of a huge city reared toward the sky. I had only time to see that the vehicles on the road, the buildings in that city, were far advanced over our own. I was going toward the city when you restarted the machine. It stopped me on the spot I was standing. When I awakened again I was here."

That was the first trip to Moneta. But we still faced many difficulties. First, how could we bring back proof that such a place really existed? I came up with an idea that, simple as it was, I thought would solve the problem. We could only bring back ideas and mental pictures. Therefore, we would gather all the information we could about the machinery, art, mathematics, etc., learned while on Moneta. Upon returning we could present that material to learned men and let them judge for themselves how successful we had been. In a like manner, every phase of life could be copied mentally and reproduced on paper when we returned. If enough people could be convinced that Moneta was really their home and far advanced over the environment imprisoned Earth, then machines like the one we had built could be made by mass production. All our finance could be diverted into transporting civilization to a new planet where a perfect future would give men and women a better life.

The plan grew in my mind until I was waiting wildly for the first chance to see Moneta for myself.

Crocket was patient. He had come so far along the right road he hated to take any risks. He went over the machine carefully, making sure that nothing could go wrong. Dan Steele came up and Crocket explained what must be done. Steele, although in danger of getting into official trouble by working with us, had promised to handle the controls and bring us back to Earth at the end of twenty-four hours. After that we would decide how long we could remain on Moneta, gathering vital material to present to the world.

Larry Keen arrived at eight in the self would fill four of the six chambers on the second trip to Moneta. Steele tightened his guard around the cottage, fearing that some maniac might manage to damage the machine. He was very deeply concerned over his responsibility.

THOROUGH checking and rechecking assured us that the direct power line that supplied the motors could not be cut off by storm or accident. The world was kept ignorant of what we planned to do so that none of our enemies could take this opportunity to get rid of us.

Larry Keen arrived at eight in the evening. He had good news.

"We held a board meeting last night," he said. "The group has raised enough cash to buy a controlling share of the *Express* from the Pinchott estate. With Pinchott himself out of the way, there isn't another power in New York that dares fight us outright. The decision of the World Congress carried a lot of weight.

"People in New York seem very deeply concerned. They are waiting for us and we've got to produce soon."

Ten o'clock was the last hour. From then on we weren't sure what we would face. If an accident occurred, it might not be pleasant. Steele had five cups of Ann's coffee. He joked nervously, like an executioner who dreads pulling the switch to the death chamber.

Larry discussed the construction of the machine with Crocket and finally gave up. Crocket's work was far beyond his understanding.

I tried to discourage Ann from going with us but she insisted. "We aren't complete unless we're together," she said. "I couldn't wait here and think of your lifeless body lying there in a metal coffin. If I'm beside you it won't bother me at all." I admitted that I felt the same, and she convinced me that she should be with us.

"Besides," she said, "I can pick up a lot of lovely future dress designs which might come in handy."

We held a council of war at ten thirty.

"We will, because of the power being uniform, and because we start together, probably find ourselves in a group on Moneta. The fact that we find ourselves in a strange world without our physical bodies should not worry us. Our thoughts will be understood by each other.

"During the first trip we will not attempt to acquire bodies. No doubt this has been arranged by the Monetians, but we'll not take advantage of it until we are sure we have all the information we will need here on Earth.

"Therefore, Steele will bring us back in twenty-four hours—to the second. We will make our plans when we reach the home planet. Is that clear?"

No one spoke. The others nodded and I followed their example.

Crocket arose.

"Good," he said. "Remember—a lot depends on us. We must remain calm and unafraid."

CHAPTER FIFTEEN
The Story of Moneta

I LAY quietly in the narrow confines of the black cabinet. Above me the Professor had taken his place. Larry, I knew, was at my right, and Ann above him. Steele slammed the glass door to my cabinet, and all sound was cut out. I'll admit it was a little frightening. I tried to relax, but my heart pounded unreasonably. It was dark. Only a dim light came from the glass near my feet. The oxygen tank was pumping fresh air into the box. I felt better.

I could feel rather than hear the throbbing of the motors. Steele was doing his job swiftly. I closed my eyes. I wasn't quite sure how much pain was in store for a man who leaves his body. There would be some sensation, I was sure, and I waited for it with a curious dread.

I was in for a surprise.

It was like sleep. A deep, dreamless sleep that comes when a mind and body are exhausted and relaxed.

Then I was awake again, and hovering over a clearing in a small grove.

Was this Moneta?

It could have been the woods near Lake Speer. The sun was bright and the day warm. I had an odd, disconnected feeling, and well might I have. It was as though my brain floated in space. I could see, and yet I could not feel. *I*, the part of me that was here, had left my body behind.

It seemed that I must only will a thing to happen and it happened. I wanted to explore the grove, and go beyond, where I could hear sounds of moving traffic. I didn't dare to leave until I contacted my friends.

"I assume that we are all here," Crocket's voice said clearly. "Although of course I can see none of you."

I heard Ann's frightened little gasp.

"I've been waiting for you," she said. "I feel fine. I didn't dare to speak out loud, afraid none of you would be here to answer me."

I felt vastly relieved.

"I'm all right," I admitted. "Although, without a body; I can see complications arising."

Larry chimed in.

"They'd have a hell of a time waging a war on Earth if everyone was as helpless as we are," he said.

Crocket sounded well pleased.

"Good—we are all here. Now, to lay definite plans for the hours we are to remain on Moneta."

Larry chuckled. "I hope Steele remembers to pull the switch," he said. "Otherwise, I want to be damned sure that they've got a body stored away for me somewhere in this new world."

He hit pretty close to the thought that worried us all. I would hate to go through life with vibrant, lovable Ann Shelton and be able to accompany her only in spirit and voice.

MENTALLY, I had already gathered many notes concerning Moneta. Our conference in the grove had been short. Crocket and Larry, or at least their mental equipment, decided to go together toward the city of spires we saw some distance away. There they would try to absorb construction details, dress designs, etc. that would impress Earth people. Ann and I were to take our time exploring the rich valley that approached the city. Here we would listen to the people when possible and find out what we could to tell the people at home.

It was a strangely beautiful scene that they gazed out upon with

It was a wonderful experience. We had no fear of being discovered for actually there was nothing to be discovered. Knowing little of the brain and the soul, I can explain it best by saying that our mental machines were on Moneta with no physical body to delay us. We had but to wish ourselves onward to a certain point and we were there without delay.

We agreed to meet in the grove well ahead of the time set by Steele for our return. In this way we would make sure that no errors occurred.

Ann suggested that we go first toward the road, for we still heard vehicles traveling on it. As Larry and Crocket had already left for the city, we started at once.

the city off in the distance and the ships rocketing overhead . . .

This valley of Moneta was a wondrous place. If this planet was as large as Earth, I thought, how can so much man-made beauty be accomplished? Yet, hadn't we decided already that Moneta was far advanced?

The highway that we approached was perhaps a hundred yards wide and its surface was as smooth as glass. The cars, for I suppose you could call them that, were propelled by powerful, soundless jets of pale blue gas that shot from the rear of the slim vehicles and vanished into the air. Speed here had been conquered, for we could hardly follow the vehicles without mental "eyes" as they shot past. Moneta was well settled, for the highway was covered at all times with a veritable tidal wave of traffic. A thousand yards away, another road carried traffic away from the city.

We drifted toward the valley, following the wide thread of the road. There were no farms here. Instead, colored glass homes were scattered about on green squares of grass. Moneta seemed a planet of color and light. The sun filled every house through soft, pastel blocks of glass. Each building was separated by several hundred yards, and the roof of every home acted as landing space for tiny, bug-like planes.

We were unable to speak to the inhabitants, but we saw many of them, that afternoon. They looked as the people of Earth do, and it was a relief to me. I had half expected some sort of four-legged green men. That's the usual conception of life on other planets.

These people of Moneta looked like your Uncle Ned and your Aunt Helen. However, their dress and their living conditions were far advanced. We saw nothing that would point to a country that lived in the past. Most of all, that was what we had come for. Environment, we were sure, had never touched here. In searching the homes, we saw that books and papers—everything spoke of and looked to the future. Nothing was wrinkled with age.

Yet this did not account for the worried expressions on the faces of the people we saw. We regretted that we could not break in on any of their conversations, for by their speech, they might give us some clue.

The people of Moneta, in spite of the jewel-like setting they lived in, were worried.

What worried them we couldn't guess. Yet, when they gathered in groups near their homes, or read their papers, it was evident that their minds were filled with a troublesome thought that they couldn't drive out. It showed in bitter little lines around their mouths and in the corners of their eyes.

UNABLE to fathom the secret, we hurried back to the grove. Professor Crocket was worried about our continued absence.

"It is very near the time for Steele to take us home," he said. "I was afraid you might not get back."

We sat and waited. The wind was warm in the grove. We were all excited over what we had seen.

"That city is perfect," Larry said with enthusiasm. "It's got everything. Elevators work on compressed air, shooting the cars three hundred stories aloft. The sun up there is wonderful. Every office absorbs it through ultraviolet screens."

"Even the basements," Crocket added, "are fitted with sun-reflectors that carry the heat and ultra-violet rays of the sun to the lowest levels. There couldn't be any disease."

"The cars that you saw on the road belong mostly to the workers." Larry couldn't forget the things he had witnessed. "Through an ingenious arrangement of road levels, a man can drive directly to his building through a service door and be lifted while still inside his car to a garage on the floor level where he works. No man or woman is more than a few steps from his car at any time."

There were other wonders, but I noticed the sudden look of uneasiness that showed on Professor Crocket's face.

"One thing worries me," he admitted, and I knew it was the same thing Ann and I had felt. "The people of Moneta aren't entirely happy."

"You know," Larry added, "I didn't say anything at the time, but I had that same feeling. They look nervous—as though they were afraid of mentioning something and yet couldn't get whatever it is off their minds."

I told them quickly that Ann and I had noticed the same thing.

"I did overhear one bit of conversation that might have applied," Larry said. "It was between a couple of men who worked high in the office system. One of them said, 'If they *do* find anything, it would affect the whole system!' "

Crocket thought, for some time, then gave up, as we had been forced to do.

"I don't know what it is," he admitted, "but never fear, we'll get to the bottom of the mystery once we come to Moneta to stay."

Come to stay?

It had a nice sound to it. Clean, super cities—colorful utopias in hidden valleys.

Then a strange emotion passed through me, and I was homesick. Homesick for the dirty, paper-strewn streets and the noisy traffic of New York. Homesick for a bowl of chili and a beer at Brett's Bar. We of Earth are foolish, tradition bound people, but the thought of walking across Times Square again had a good feel to it. Poison spouting automobiles were screaming their mechanical lungs out. Men and women were spitting and breathing in each other's faces, where the sun seldom shone. Perhaps we were meant for that life, and not for the perfection of Moneta? I wondered.

The returning sensation was very pleasant. One moment we were busy talking over what we had seen and locking it all carefully in our memory. The next, a strange drowsy sensation passed through us all and we awakened feeling heavy and a little strange, once more locked in the bodies we had left on Earth. I was still unaccustomed to my load when Dan Steele, relief showing plainly in his eyes, helped me from the cabinet of Professor Crocket's wonderful machine.

THE day after our return to Earth, Larry Keen insisted that all four of us fly to New York. We went at once to the offices of the *Express*. I noticed a strange, subtle difference in the city since I had gone to Lake Speer. Laughter had vanished. Everyone seemed to look a little frightened. Unanswered questions were on every man's face.

What would Professor Crocket have to say to a curious waiting world?

In the art department, each of us was turned over to a staff artist and a reporter. It felt fine, giving, instead of taking a story, for a change. For three hours I made suggestions and answered questions shot at me by both men. I knew that Crocket and Ann were doing the same thing. Larry was in his office, hard at work with the top artist in town. When he emerged, the entire city we had visited on Moneta would be on canvas.

I explained the general appearance of the valley, the homes, and the living conditions. The artists worked hard, checking with each other concerning details. At one o'clock in the afternoon, the work was done. The *Express* tomorrow morning would carry the complete word and picture story of Moneta in its pages.

Every copy was sold out in advance.

By three in the afternoon, tele-photo had reproduced every sketch and sent them all over the world. Professor Crockett gave technical explanations of how many of Moneta's marvels were based on theories never before suggested by Earth scientists. These facts would prove beyond a doubt that no one man could invent the story. We knew that men and women would read and believe what they read. That was important.

CHAPTER SIXTEEN
I Satisfy a Terrible Doubt

I'LL never forget the day that followed. *At last the world believed.* There was no doubt this time. Crocket had impressed the World Congress, and now every man of any importance stepped forward to fight at his side.

At nine in the morning the President of the United States read a short address, broadcast in seven different languages to all points in the world. I will never forget his closing words.

"There is no doubt that James Crocket has discovered a secret that has held us bound in tradition for centuries. I cannot comment on whether this is good or bad. I don't care to express myself on a problem that concerns the people themselves, and therefore should be answered in each mind according to that person's own common sense. However," he paused, "I have talked by trans-oceanic telephone with London and Moscow. We agree that Professor James Crocket is a man who has been working for the betterment of civilization. He will be interviewed by a committee chosen from the United Nations. If he wishes to share his knowledge with the Axis nations he will be given that privilege. Perhaps the people of Earth will demand a mass migration to the home planet of Moneta. I cannot make such a decision. It is up to you. There is plenty of time. Think well, America, and you of other nations. This may be your opportunity to find a warless Utopia. It may bring happiness everlasting and allow you to escape a world that has not been a very happy place for many years."

That was all. It was a straightforward speech. I had no doubt about the decision that people would reach sooner or later. Moneta was too appealing—too wonderful to miss. Perhaps only a few would go at first. Then, when others saw their friends moving into a Utopia they had all dreamed of, they would follow. The world would be left, an isolated crude globe, spinning in space. Four footed animals and creatures of the water would come into their rightful heritage and rule a man-less world.

But first I had a task to perform.

Perhaps it was my newspaper training that would not let me rest.

Professor Crocket spent the next two weeks rushing from one conference to another. He was in London on Monday, and when Thursday came around, we received a cable from Cairo.

"Meeting Russian, English, and African officials here," he said. "Mass migration system planned. Machine all set for production in seven key cities."

Inside of another month, Crocket's machine would be on the assembly line all over the world. Perhaps, if nothing occurred to stop the plan, Earth would be deserted before another Christmas came around.

But Johnny Sharp has a nose for news. It isn't an exceptionally pretty nose, but it gets around and Ann Shelton likes it. That's why, on Saturday night, after we heard that Crocket was en route to China to meet Chiang Kai-shek, she and I retreated to the laboratory at Lake Speer and carefully locked the door. I explained once more how the machine was operated, found myself locked in one of the upper cabinets and waited for Ann to pull the switch.

I had one more task to perform on Moneta, before Crocket launched his full-scale migration to that planet.

To my wonder and delight I came to Moneta when light was hanging like a dark velvet over the valley. Never have I seen anything to compare with the sight I saw from the edge of the highway. The city, in fact every dwelling in the valley that approached the city, was glowing with colors of the rainbow. I suppose it was caused by the colored glass that these homes and offices were constructed of. Pale greens, blues, pinks—every shade of spectrum danced and reflected over the darkened countryside. Above, the sky was bright with strange stars that of course I hadn't yet become accustomed to. I had no idea, nor did Crocket, where Moneta was actually located, in relation to the other planets.

Our problem had been one of mental travel, rather than flying.

WE COULD face one question at a time, and once the population of Earth came here, they would find out the answers to questions as yet unexpressed.

But the valley *was* perfect and everything about Moneta pleased me more than it had during the first trip.

But I had a job to do and do it I must. The future would depend on my research on Moneta. I couldn't fail.

I searched carefully that night, fighting my exhausted mind to go on—to listen for some word that would confirm what I thought I knew.

Close to morning I found the solution.

I followed the highway away from the city—far from the valley we first saw. I travelled through other valleys and visited other cities, each more perfect than the first. Then a sight met my eye that made my heart pound with excitement.

I wasn't sure of myself. What was I actually looking for? I left the highway and hurried toward a single ugly scar in the surface of the planet. I knew the answer was within my reach.

Perhaps a half mile from the road, I saw a deep excavation. When I reached it, I saw that it measured about a mile long and half as wide. It went deep, and at the bottom, I saw rugged stone, up thrust from the soft dirt. Men with baskets on their shoulders toiled up steep slopes from the hole. They dumped their dirt on screens, where others sifted the stuff carefully, occasionally removing bits of rock and other material.

I dropped down, coming close to the men at the screens. They worked slowly, painstakingly. Their eyes were narrowed with excitement and their faces showed the wonder that was in their minds. I could hear two of them, one a very old man with white sideburns, talking urgently as they worked.

"I think this bit of stone will date back to the quartz age," he said. "You recall our Professor mentioning that the quartz workers were excellent warriors?"

The younger man had keen eyes and long, searching fingers. He took the bit of quartz eagerly. His voice was high pitched.

"This is wonderful!" He sounded so deeply impressed that I wondered if the work was new to him. "It will shed new light on our ancestors."

New light on our ancestors. But, I thought, you have no ancestors. That is what makes Moneta such a wonderful place. You should not delve into the past. You should look to the future or you will become bound by environment as surely as Earth's men have.

"Take my word for it, Herod," the old man said, "we will dig deeper and we will find the secret of the Wars of Piras. The men of his age fought brilliantly. It will be a feather in our cap if we show the High Council how Piras fought. His technique was flawless."

Wars on Moneta? It was unthinkable. Here was Utopia, untouched by bloodshed.

Yet this was why I had come back. It was the thing I had feared.

I left the pair and went into the depths of the pit. Here, other men grubbed in the dirt with small spades. They arose occasionally, picking up slabs of rock. On the rocks were inscriptions. Messages from the past. Messages that had intrigued men of Earth and *tied* them to the past.

I could hear the people of Moneta, when they found out that during other ages, a man named Piras had made war a glorious pastime, fighting it for the pleasure derived from killing.

"We have everything," they would say. *"Yet are we happy? There have been wars before. Perhaps we should take things from our neighbors as Piras did. Perhaps war is inevitable. Perhaps we were not meant to escape it."*

I shuddered. I was dreaming and yet…was I? The men and women of Moneta were worried. About this?

VOICE close by startled me and I turned to see a bearded ancient arise with a strip of rusted metal in his hands. He held the thing aloft, shaking it in both hands. His voice was shrill.

"What will those milksops of the Peace Legation say when we place this wondrous weapon on their desk? What will they answer when we say:

"This is the battle sword of Piras, and we can dig more truth from the planet's surface. We can dig until we prove that Moneta has a heritage. A wonderful heritage to be preserved at any cost."

They flocked to his side, hiding him from me, but I heard one of his companions speak:

"The councilors fought to make us give up what they called *useless scraping at the surface of a virgin Earth."* he shouted. "Now the council will find that we have a past. A past of wonderful wars and savage nations. This excavation will become the first sight of *true* knowledge."

Disgust filled me. It made me want to run back to the spot where the machine had placed me and wait for Ann to take me home.

I was witnessing the beginning of the end of Utopia. The people had become curious. They had succeeded in building wonderful things, because they had not been chained by wars and heartaches of the past. These men I watched were spoiling for all time the opportunity that Moneta had to be the perfect planet.

I knew now that I was correct in guessing the reason for so much unhappiness. The people waited anxiously for knowledge these men were bringing to the surface.

Moneta, I knew at that moment, would be no better and no worse than Earth. Men should not come here, for they would face the very things they sought to escape. Professor Crocket had been right, but now, because Moneta had forgotten the very reason for its success, it was, in a sense, doomed.

For man has fortified himself behind the complete alibi. He found a reason why he should fight wars.

He knows that it has all happened before, and instead of fighting against these conditions, he remarks smugly that history repeats itself.

Moneta had a history now, and it was sure to repeat itself.

I turned away, blind with anger against the men in the pit.

I faced the greatest decision of my life. It wasn't pleasant, but there was no other way to prevent the vast migration plan from going through. Ann understood me and forgave me for what I did.

I knew that I could not undo the things that had been done. Professor Crocket was so firmly entrenched that even if he denied his own story, people would say that he was selfish and would go ahead by themselves to establish new colonies on Moneta.

I had one escape. I wired the full story to Crocket, telling him what I had found out and how I had decided to proceed. It was sent in code, as the President and the Army approved of my plan. I received his reply at once, saying he would leave by clipper, notifying all the leaders of the world of his actions.

Then I called Larry Keen. We spent seven hours sweating out the story that might spell the end to the *Daily Express*.

Of course this story was circulated throughout the world and the people were furious. In the long run, people forget and forgive very easily. Professor Crocket joined Ann and myself. We packed quietly, destroyed the machine, and ran away to a remote lake north of the Canadian border.

Crocket was deeply hurt and yet he realized that men of science knew the true story. It was only the people who believed the article Larry and I had prepared.

For we had announced to the world that Professor Crocket was mad. That we had been taken in by his story, until, on our own initiative, we had tried out his machine. We exposed Moneta as being a product of the Professor's warped mind, claiming that he convinced us through mass hypnotism, Larry wired us a week later, and the wire was delivered to us with the supplies that came in by canoe:

New York has forgiven Express. Circulation up hundred percent. Congress of Science has full story and wants Crocket on their staff in London. You and Ann better stay hidden for month. When you return New York, have job Managing Editor for you. I'm moving into Johnson's office. Kisses to Ann.

Larry.

CHAPTER SEVENTEEN
Memory Is Elusive.

NEEDLESS to say, Crocket left at once for London. Before he went out with the guide, Ann and I were married. I forgot to mention that the guide was Father Jeffries, a priest who lived at the remote trading post.

Ann and I stayed out our month with pleasure.

When we left the lake, Ann had a huge scrapbook of new designs, all taken from Moneta and her people.

We visited Barney Slocum's grave a few days later, and I stood there with my hat off, talking to Barney like a kid. I told him everything that had happened and thanked him once more for being a great guy. Ann was crying when she placed a bouquet of roses near the headstone.

"I wonder if he'll like them," she asked softly. "He wasn't really such a tough guy."

Moneta, since those days, has grown into another Lost World story. Occasionally the subject comes up in some Sunday Supplement, but the *Express* steadfastly refuses to comment on it in any way. Crocket is deep in research work now, but he depends on Moneta for most of his scientific theories.

I received a long letter from him last week. The letter caused me to publish this account. In part, this is what he had to say:

"Moneta is still alive. Behind locked doors, Waterman, Bruck, and myself have worked stubbornly with the *Memory Finder*. We managed to isolate and bring to Earth a man of Moneta! We placed him under the *Memory Finder*, hoping to find out once and for all what really happened in years past on that planet.

"This will amaze you. The man spoke clearly and intelligently upon several subjects, yet failed to remember anything about the Earth experiment. *When the Memory Finder was set back to 1925, his mind became a complete blank.*

"This leaves us exactly where we started. Moneta has no history beyond the time that Earth people can remember. Can we, on this basis, say that both Moneta and Earth face the same problem? It sounds incredible, but are both planets an experiment, perhaps conceived by a third, still more perfect civilization? I shall spend my life trying to find out. The thought is perhaps beyond the end of the trail that my mind is capable of following."

The idea frightens me. How far must we progress, to find the perfection we seek? If we did find it, would we be entirely happy?

"What a book a devil's chaplain might write on the clumsy, wasteful, blundering, low, and horribly cruel works of nature." —Charles Darwin.

THE END

Made in the USA
Middletown, DE
25 September 2022

10855503R00130